"It's beautiful!" She turned onto a small black-topped area and sucked in her breath as she stopped the vehicle. They were on top of the world! Miles and miles of pine-covered mountains, deep valleys, and brilliant stars surrounded them. "How did you find this place?"

"I come up here sometimes just to get my perspective on the world back."

She glanced away from the view. "Is your perspective out again?"

Not tonight. There's another reason why I wanted to come here tonight."

She noticed how serious he was and wondered if she was about to be fired. "What's that?"

"I want to kiss you."

She laughed with relief. "You made me drive you all the way up here just so you could kiss me?"

"I didn't want to kiss you at home."

"Why not?"

"Because I don't want you to think me kissing you has anything to do with our arrangement. If you don't want me to kiss you, just say so, and we'll pretend this never happened."

She unsnapped her seat belt. "What do we do if I want to kiss you back?"

WHAT ARE *LOVESWEPT* ROMANCES?

They are stories of true romance and touching emotion. We believe those two very important ingredients are constants in our highly sensual and very believable stories in the LOVE-SWEPT line. Our goal is to give you, the reader, stories of consistently high quality that may sometimes make you laugh, sometimes make you cry, but are always fresh and creative and contain many delightful surprises within their pages.

Most romance fans read an enormous number of books. Those they truly love, they keep. Others may be traded with friends and soon forgotten. We hope that each LOVESWEPT romance will be a treasure—a "keeper." We will always try to publish

LOVE STORIES YOU'LL NEVER FORGET BY AUTHORS YOU'LL ALWAYS REMEMBER

The Editors

Loveswept ® *818*

TANGLED UP IN BLUE

MARCIA
EVANICK

BANTAM BOOKS

NEW YORK · TORONTO · LONDON · SYDNEY · AUCKLAND

TANGLED UP IN BLUE

A Bantam Book / January 1997

ISBN 0-553-44562-6

Published simultaneously in the United States and Canada

Bantam Books are published by Bantam Books, a division of Bantam
Doubleday Dell Publishing Group, Inc. Its trademark, consisting of the
words "Bantam Books" and the portrayal of a rooster, is Registered in U.S.
Patent and Trademark Office and in other countries. Marca Registrada.
Bantam Books, 1540 Broadway, New York, New York 10036.

PRINTED IN THE UNITED STATES OF AMERICA

OPM   0 9 8 7 6 5 4 3 2 1

*A good rule for going through
life is to keep the heart a little
softer than the head.*

ONE

There was something deliriously sinful about floating naked in a private swimming pool on the hottest night in August.

The silver shimmer of the pool had proved too great a temptation for Beulah—Blue to her friends—Crawford. She had walked through the sliding door onto the wooden deck and thought about going back inside for her bathing suit. But who was going to see her? She was miles from anywhere on a mountain in Vermont. Without bothering to turn on the outside lights, she had shed her clothes and dived into the cool water. Heaven. After her third lap she'd turned onto her back and floated under the stars.

Two months earlier the still water would have made her dream of mermaids, Captain Nemo, and all the fascinating sea creatures she remembered from childhood books. Tonight her thoughts were on more adult fantasies: chilled champagne, long slow kisses, black satin sheets, and the absent Matthew Stone.

She had been living in Matthew Stone's house for two months now, and would be staying until his return next May. He was the perfect man to be fantasizing about. For eight weeks she had been learning a great deal about the man who had built this wonderful log home on top of a mountain. Matt was single, well traveled—if the unusual collection of cheap, if not gaudy, souvenirs in the guest bedroom was any indication—and comfortably well-off. He valued his privacy, pampered his two cats, and was totally absorbed in the mystical world of computers. Except for that last bit, he was the perfect lover to dream about.

Nothing flustered her more than computers, except for cooking. Give her a missing engine and she could troubleshoot it within minutes, but ask her to sauté some onions and she would screw it up every time. Computers held the same mystique as a food processor, a magical invention to be handled only by the gods. Over the past several years Blue had watched a few cooking shows, trying to gain some knowledge, but only came away more frustrated. All the great cooks talked with foreign accents and preached the gospel of gourmet cooking with more zeal than a Baptist preacher predicting doom and hellfires for sinners. Why couldn't PBS air a show that explained how to fry an egg, bake a cake from a box mix, or boil water without scorching the pot?

Computer shows hadn't made their way to the ever-expanding world of television yet, but Blue was sure they would. Computers were everywhere else. A person could now pay her bills, install a security system, and figure out her most fertile time of the month, all without ever leaving her keyboard. The age of *The Jetsons* was approaching faster than Blue liked. It wouldn't be too bad if only she could afford a mechanical robot named Rosie, and if all she had to do was push a button, and voilà, instant food.

Computers were even taking over in the college classrooms. If she didn't hurry up and graduate, her dream of becoming a teacher might be obsolete. All a child would need would be a computer with a CD-ROM and the world would be his for the taking.

Blue closed her eyes and blocked out the star-studded sky. She wasn't going to dwell on anything negative tonight. Landing this plum housesitting job had been a godsend, an answer to her dreams. Tonight especially, she should be out celebrating. That afternoon she had registered and paid for the fall semester at Bennington College. By May she would have enough credits to graduate and her dream would finally be within reach. She was going to become a teacher, and computers be damned.

She floated in the darkness and allowed the cool water to soothe her battered soul. So many years. So many setbacks. At last it was all within her grasp.

Matthew Stone painfully climbed out of the taxi and stared at his house. Home. He was finally home after twelve hours of flights and layovers. Except for a light burning in the living room, the huge modern house of logs and glass was in total darkness.

"Hey, buddy, do you want me to carry in your luggage?" asked the driver.

Matt muttered an obscenity as he accidentally placed all his weight on his bad leg. "Yes, please," he said as he reached for his crutches. He positioned the crutches under his arms and hobbled to the garage. Peering inside, he saw only the dark outline of his Bronco. Beulah, the housesitter, must be out somewhere.

Why had he agreed to allow a total stranger to stay in his home? he wondered as he made his way to the front door. He had felt funny leaving for Germany before even meeting Beulah Crawford. She had come highly praised by the agency, and Jared, his best friend, had called two days after Matt had left Vermont to assure him that Beulah was taking excellent care of his home and two cats. Still, she was a stranger living among his things.

Usually when he had to go out of town on business, it was only for a couple of days, a week or two at the most. The trip to Germany would have been his crowning achievement. Jared always watered his plants, took care of his cats, and kept an eye on the fortune of computer equipment while he was away. The job in Germany was to have lasted nearly a year, though. He couldn't leave his house empty for that long, so he had contacted an agency for a housesitter.

Why in the hell had he accepted the job in the first place? he asked himself as he searched his pockets for his keys. For the past several years, he had avoided traveling. With modern technology he could do most of his work at home, which suited him just fine. He had a natural-born gift for computers. There wasn't a system or program he couldn't figure out, fix, or create. So when a prestigious German automobile manufacturer had contacted him, explaining their plans to expand into America and that they needed his skills in setting up a computer system geared for the U.S. that would also be compatible with their existing system, he hadn't been able to refuse.

The money they had offered him was more than substantial, but he hadn't taken the job for the financial benefits. It had been for the challenge, the new experience of merging two countries' technologies and all the opportunities that would present him in the future.

Only in the darkest hours would he admit to himself that he had also taken the assignment because he was bored. The traveling bug his mother had planted in him as a small boy had reared its ugly head at the same time the German company had contacted him. It was a horrible coincidence, and one he hoped would never happen again.

The taxi driver piled his three suitcases inside the front door. He eyed the crutches and the grimace of pain on Matt's face. "Are you sure you're going to be all right here?"

Matt pulled out his wallet and handed the man his fare plus a generous tip. It was a long drive from the airport in Albany, New York, to the southwestern corner of Vermont. "I'll be fine, thanks." His leg was throbbing and aching after the three different flights, but he was home. His home.

The thought of meeting the unknown Beulah Crawford brought a frown to his brow. Jared hadn't described her, so Matt had conjured up his own image of her. Her name sounded old-fashioned, with a hint of Southern charm. She would be in her late sixties, he'd decided, white-haired, sipped mint-julep tea, and could outbake the Pillsbury Dough Boy. Beulah was probably down at Greenhaven's Volunteer Fire Hall playing bingo with the rest of the senior citizens of the small rural town.

He closed the door behind the taxi driver and glanced around his living room. He was relieved to see everything was exactly the way he had left it, except for a few magazines scattered on the coffee table and a light film of dust covering everything. Although the dust was a little out of character for his Beulah, she appeared to be as dependable as Jared had promised.

The only light was from the lamp next to the couch. The rest of the house was shrouded in darkness. Good, he thought. He was alone. He was turning toward the pile of luggage when the silver reflection of the in-ground pool caught his attention. A dip would feel like heaven after so many hours of torturous flying and waiting for connections. His leg was one throbbing mass of trembling muscles. The doctors at the Berlin hospital, where he had been operated on, had made him promise to check in with a doctor as soon as he arrived home, and to exercise the leg regularly. Swimming was excellent exercise, and maybe it would relieve some of the tension in his leg so he would be able to sleep that night.

The crutches took most of his weight as he eased open the sliding doors and limped onto the deck. Two thirds of the swimming pool was hidden in darkness, but the part he could see looked cool and inviting. Gingerly, he made his way down the five steps to the lower deck. Pausing there, he gave a passing thought to his swimming trunks. He could only hope Beulah didn't return soon, or if she did, that the old gal had a strong heart or at least a sense of humor. It would take more than the possibility of being caught skinny-dipping for him to climb back up the stairs and search through three suitcases to locate his bathing suit.

Holding on to a recliner, he stripped off every stitch of clothing. With the help of one crutch he reached the shallow steps in the pool without killing himself.

Cautiously, he lowered himself into a sitting position. Cool water covered his feet and lapped at his calves, promising relief to the rest of his tired, hot body. He laid the crutch on the deck behind him, sucked in a deep breath, and made a most undignified entrance into the water.

The splash jolted Blue out of her daydream. She was not alone anymore. One quick glance confirmed the fact that there was a huge shape in the shallow end, and fear crept up her spine. Knowing she was the sole human for miles around, only one thought flashed through her mind. Bear!

Her bloodcurdling scream echoed off the water, the house, and the surrounding forest. The dark shape seemed to turn in her direction, then a deep masculine voice yelled, "Stop that!"

Blue reached the farthest edge of the pool at the same instant the human voice registered. She hauled herself partially out of the pool before she remembered the only thing she was wearing was a golden ankle bracelet. Glancing over her shoulder, she saw the shape had not moved since he had yelled. She knew she was virtually invisible in the darkness, so she slid slowly back into the water to contemplate her options.

As the last echo of her scream faded into the distance, the man at the other end of the pool demanded, "Who in the hell are you?"

"I live here. Who in the hell are you?" she demanded right back.

"Beulah Crawford?"

Blue peered at the barely visible head. If he knew who she was, he must be a friend of Jared so considering her attire, or lack thereof, she decided to stall. "You don't sound like a Beulah," she said.

"Your mother must have had a hell of a labor to name you Beulah." When all she heard was a distant muttering, she continued, "Maybe you're one of those transsexuals I've heard about. Have you ever been on the *Oprah* show?"

"Beulah, stuff it."

She sank her teeth into her lower lip. He sounded irritated, maybe even in pain, but who was he? "You seem to have me at a disadvantage. You know my name, but I don't know yours."

"Sorry I startled you, Beulah." As if he'd just realized how shocking his sudden appearance was to her, he spoke in a softer voice. "I'm Matthew Stone."

"You're not due back until next May."

"I had a slight accident."

Blue thought that one through. What would a computer nerd consider a "slight accident," a paper cut? Okay, so the wizard of the keyboard was back home early. She could handle that. The man whose home she had been living in for the past eight weeks had returned. She could handle that. She was totally naked in his pool with him. That she couldn't handle. "I'm sorry to hear about your accident," she said, her voice quivering in the night air.

Matt knew he had made a major miscalculation. That voice floating across the darkness to him did not belong to an aging Beulah who baked cookies, served tea, and talked about the South rising again. No, her voice made him think of lovers in the dark. Satin on satin. Skin on skin. Promises to be kept. Secrets to be shared. With a shake of his head, he muttered, "Nothing I can't handle."

"Why don't you go on in?" she said. "I'll be right there."

He chuckled and glanced down into the darkened depths of the pool. "Beulah, I think you should go in first. I'll join you in a few minutes."

"No one's ever called me Beulah but my father. Call me Blue."

"Blue?" What kind of name was Blue? "The first thing is, it's going to be awkward for me to get out of this pool and I would rather not have an audience. The second is, the only thing I'm wearing is a watch." When all he heard was a muffled "Oh!" Matt chuckled.

An uncomfortable minute ticked by while he wondered what she was thinking. "Blue, aren't you going to let me do the gentlemanly thing? Go ahead in. I'll join you as soon as I can manage to haul myself out of the water and into some clothes."

"I seemed to have forgotten something," she said at last.

"What's that?"

"My swimsuit."

This time it was his turn to mutter "Oh!" Matt ran a hand through his damp hair. Oh, Lord! That sexy voice was naked. That voice that made promises only a male would understand was naked and in his pool. The pain in his thigh was forgotten as heat shot across his abdomen. Great, he was getting aroused by the voice of a woman he had never even seen.

Another awkward minute passed before she said, "Okay, Matt, I'll go in first." She hesitated, then added, "Do you need any help getting out of the pool?"

"No. You go ahead in." When he heard her pull herself out of the water, he called upon every ounce of self-control he had and closed his eyes. He forced himself to go under and swim toward the deep end of the pool.

A moment later Matt surfaced silently just as Blue reached her pile of clothes. It was a good thing he had taken a deep breath before locating her, because his mind temporarily shut down every function except sight and need as soon as he saw her.

The living-room light shone through the sliding doors, turning the water that was clinging to her to a sparkling golden sheen. She was turned away from him, and he had a view of a shapely back, a pert bottom, and a stunning pair of legs. As Blue raised her arms over her head to pull on her T-shirt, he glimpsed the silhouette of firm high breasts. The shirt fell to just below her bottom as she shook out her wild mass of curly hair.

Matt bit his knuckles to keep from groaning aloud when she bent over to retrieve her shorts. Without a backward glance, she climbed the wooden steps to the upper deck and disappeared into the living room. Matt slowly took the knuckles from between his teeth and stared up at the sliver of moon. He wondered if there were any werewolves in his family, because he suddenly felt like howling.

Blue grabbed clean clothes from her bureau and fumed. He had peeked. She had felt his eyes on her just as she'd slipped on the T-shirt. The sneak! After entering the bathroom, she locked the door; Matthew Stone was definitely not a gentleman. The little computer nerd had gotten a cheap thrill, at her expense. That was what she got for fantasizing about him while floating naked in his pool. If he was still alive, her father would have told her it was her punishment for having wicked thoughts of the flesh. Then again, if Neville Crawford was still alive, he would be making sure she didn't have time for wicked thoughts.

Blue allowed the warm water of the shower to wash away any thoughts of her father. Neville Crawford was out of her life and seeking his reward in Paradise. She closed her eyes and prayed her father had finally found some peace. For herself, she had a more pressing problem to dwell on, besides the past.

Mr. Computer Whiz had returned a heckuva lot sooner than expected. She did a rough calculation of her money situation and groaned. If she pinched every penny she had, and took on a couple more hours a week at the restaurant she was working in, she could possibly make it through this semester. But that would leave her one full semester away from graduating. The free board of Matt's home was supposed to have lasted until she had the diploma in her hands. Still, Matt's early arrival wasn't the worst thing that had ever happened to her. She'd had more major setbacks on her quest for her dream. But it sure had felt wonderful dreaming about graduating in May.

She stepped out of the shower and vigorously rubbed herself dry. Dropping the towel, she looked at herself critically in the mirror. Her large blue eyes, which often held a faraway dreamy look, stared back. Wet golden curls clung together in their attempt to become tangled. A turned-up nose sprinkled with freckles screamed out "cute." Add one mouth that had a tendency to turn up at the corners even when she was angry, and what did you get? Wholesome. Ugh! She hated wholesome.

She wrinkled her nose as she blow-dried her hair into its normal tousled style and wondered how seriously Matt had injured himself. Was it bad enough to keep him home? Or was he there for a brief R&R before going right back to Germany? She brightened at the thought. If that was the case, maybe he would allow her to stay. Where was it Jared Miller, Matt's friend, had told her Matt was? Berlin? Berlin sounded like a wonderful city. A city she would love to visit one day. A city Matt might be returning to shortly.

With a determined smile, she left the bathroom to prove to Matthew Stone that she was the best housesitter he'd ever encountered. As she passed through the guest bedroom she noticed the unmade bed, her clothes dropped on the chair by the window, and a pair of bunny slippers peeking out from under the bed. Great. The lord and master returned wounded to the nest, only to discover it had been turned into a pigsty. Some housesitter she was.

She heard the shower running in the master bedroom as she made her way downstairs, and smiled again. If he had made his way upstairs, Matt couldn't be hurt too badly. She entered the kitchen with her mind made up. She would ignore the fact that the little weasel had peeked if he was heading directly back to Germany.

Ten minutes later Blue heard the sound of footsteps slowly descending the stairs as she was trying to decide how many scoops of coffee to use. The glass container was marked for ten cups, so she dumped ten heaping scoops of Colombia's finest into the paper filter and added a full pitcher of water. Just as she was turning away from the counter, Matthew Stone hobbled into the kitchen.

Blue had expected him to look like a dweeb. She'd thought a computer whiz would be slight in build and wearing thick glasses and a white button-down collar shirt with a nerd pack stuck in the pocket. Instead she encountered a powerful chest encased in a dark green T-shirt. Her gaze traveled down to take in a trim waist and faded jeans hugging narrow hips. Powerful thighs led into long legs that ended in a pair of bare feet. She noticed all his weight was resting on one leg while the other was bent, with the foot raised off the white-and-blue tiled floor. Planted next to the sexiest toes Blue had ever had the pleasure to meet were the red plastic tips of crutches.

Startled, she looked up at his face. Eyes the color of expensive brandy stared back. His chestnut hair was carelessly brushed, but it was clear he'd had an expensive cut. His face was not boyishly handsome, but attractive in its maturity. Matt stood over six feet and had the body of a Northern woodsman. For a fleeting moment Blue was positive that despite his commanding appearance, there was something vulnerable about him. Something more than the hurt leg and his dependence on the crutches.

Smiling, she stuck out her hand and said, "Hi, I'm Blue. You must be Matt."

Matt watched as Blue walked toward him with hand outstretched, and for an insane instant he wanted to run. This was the woman who had been living in his house for the past eight weeks? She barely reached five-two, and if she weighed much over a hundred pounds, it was when she was soaking wet. A riot of golden curls bounced in every direction, and eyes the color of the morning sky sparkled. Her most enticing feature was her mouth. Sensational lips seemed to smile just for him.

Why in the hell wasn't she some lacy-collar, apron-wearing old maid?

He braced his right crutch against his side and

held out his hand. "Glad to meet you, Blue. Sorry I gave you such a fright out in the pool. I thought I had the house to myself." He felt his hand swallow her smaller, delicate one. A shiver of awareness slid down his back. He hastily released her hand and glanced around the kitchen to hide his reaction. He had been attracted to women before, but not so instantly.

"That's okay," she said. "I thought I was alone too. Would you like a cup of coffee?"

"Great." Matt made his way to the kitchen table. "So how are the cats?"

"Oh, you mean the animals that empty the bowl of cat food every night? Jared said there were two." Blue poured two cups of coffee.

"Yeah, Moondancer and Raven."

She carried the cups to the table. "Well, I don't know how to break this to you, but I have never seen them. They eat their food each night and on occasion they leave behind a dead rodent."

Matt chuckled as he envisioned this wild-haired enchantress disposing of the remains. She did not seem overly concerned, while most women would have been repulsed, at the least.

"Sorry about that. It's their way of showing appreciation."

"Cute." Blue blew across the top of her coffee. "What happened to your leg?"

"I was just in the wrong place at the wrong time," Matt replied nonchalantly. When he noticed she still appeared interested, he added, "Some drunk decided he owned the whole road and the taxi I was riding in happened to get in his way. He smashed into the door I was sitting next to, and some metal part of the door embedded itself in one of the muscles in my thigh and damaged an artery."

Blue shuddered. "Ouch. Are you going to be okay?"

"Yes. After a three-hour operation to patch the artery and repair the torn muscle, I had to spend five days in the hospital. I then had to sit for a week in the apartment I had just rented waiting for the doctors to give me permission to fly home. They assured me that with plenty of exercise and regular checkups I should be dancing by Christmas."

"Sounds promising."

She obviously wasn't the fussy type, Matt mused, though he wasn't sure whether that pleased him or not. He glanced around the kitchen. A couple of dirty dishes were sitting in the sink and a half-eaten package of chocolate-chip cookies was lying open on the counter. "Do you have any food in the house?" he asked hopefully. "I haven't eaten since my layover in London."

She looked around the room herself, but as if in a panic. Her sky-blue eyes seemed anxious with a shadowing of dread. As if someone was forcing her to do something against her will. She looked back at him. "How about some scrambled eggs?"

"Sounds great, if it isn't too much trouble." He watched her rise and walk over to the refrigerator. As she opened the door and bent over, Matt took his first mouthful of coffee. Fiery liquid burned its way down his throat. His eyeballs clung precariously to their sockets while his taste buds committed hara-kiri.

When air reentered his lungs, Matt gingerly set the cup down, careful not to spill a drop in fear of taking the varnish off the table. Was that supposed to be coffee? If so, it was the worst he had ever tasted.

He watched Blue take out a frying pan, bowl, a carton of eggs, and the salt and pepper. As she cracked six eggs into the large bowl, added a dash of milk, salt, and pepper, Matt started to relax. She seemed to know what she was doing when it came to eggs. Coffee obviously was another story.

Four minutes later she set a plate of eggs down in front of him, along with the salt and pepper. If he ignored the dark brown edges, the eggs looked perfectly normal. Deciding not to take another chance on the coffee, he asked, "May I please have a glass of milk?"

"Sure." She poured the milk and sat across from him. "So, are you home for good, or are you going back?"

"Home for good. Someone else will be given the job." He watched the pleasant smile fade from her face.

"I guess I should go pack, then."

He stiffened in surprise. She was going to leave. He hadn't had time to think of all the ramifications his accident would cause. He had completely forgotten his housesitter until he had been heading up his driveway in the back of the taxi. He scooped up a forkful of eggs and asked, "Where will you go?"

"There's a little motel on the edge of town, Tony's Place."

"Tony's Place?" Tony's Place was one step up from being a dive. "Don't you have a home to go to?" He forced himself not to grimace as he chewed the mouthful of crunchy eggs.

Blue stared into her coffee cup. "That's why I'm a housesitter, Matt. I don't have a house of my own."

"What about your parents? Brothers or sisters?"

"No brothers or sisters. My mother died when I was ten, and my father died two years ago."

Matt took a huge swallow of milk to wash the eggs down his throat. Lord, she didn't have a family! He, at least, had a mother, even if she did live over two thousand miles away. "I'm sorry."

Blue shrugged. "All in the past, Matt. All in the past."

He pushed his fork through the eggs. Seeing nothing but eggs, he proceeded to take another mouthful. He didn't like the past, didn't like talking about it, especially his own. "So my coming home early really screwed things up for you?"

She watched as he chewed his second forkful. "Don't worry about it, Matt. Accidents happen. I'll be fine."

After swallowing, Matt knew it was not his imagination, there was something crunchy in the eggs. Casting a quick glance over toward the counter, he started to count shells. Four halves. That equaled two eggs. "Really?"

"Yeah."

"You don't sound too sure of your answer."

"I'm a big girl, Matt. I can take care of myself." She picked up her coffee and took her first sip.

Matt saw the shock register on her face as her taste buds probably screamed in agony. Thankful that at least she did not consider the coffee normal, he went back to counting eggshells.

"Does the coffee taste a little strong to you?" she asked. "I'm not used to brewing coffee. I usually throw a teaspoon of instant into a cup."

Classifying the coffee as a little strong was a joke. If the Colombians knew what she had just done to their richest, most aromatic blend, they would halt all bean exports. He shuddered thinking what that one mouthful must have cost his internal organs. "I usually only use five level scoops for the whole pot."

"That explains it."

He watched as she glanced out the window, into the night. When no other explanation was forthcoming he went back to counting shells. When he totaled twelve halves, six eggs, he gave up and took another determined mouthful of eggs. Whoever heard of fixing someone six eggs? After swallowing a large gulp of milk, he asked, "What do you do?" He'd already ruled out chef, and housesitter couldn't be a full-time occupation.

"A little of this. A little of that."

Matt nearly choked. It was the same job description his mother gave when anyone asked her what she did for a living. "Sounds like you're employed by the Mafia."

She chuckled. "I'm putting myself through college."

He nodded with understanding. Now it was making some sense. "Doing anything it takes, including being a housesitter?"

"Hey, it puts a roof over my head and leaves my money for more important things, like food and tuition."

He grimaced, remembering his college days. The long and lonely nights when he worked at some sleazebag hotel, charging the customers by the hour while cramming for the next day's exams. The lost weekends when he studied sixteen hours straight and lived on coffee and dreams. It looked like Blue was reaching for the same dream. He wondered what courses she was taking and why it had taken her so long to reach for the dream. At thirty-four, he had labeled himself a dirty old man for drooling over Blue down at the pool. Now, in the bright light of the kitchen, he could see she was on the downside of her twenties, and probably had a good seven to ten years on her fellow classmates. "Are you going to college around here?" he asked.

"I just registered at Bennington College this afternoon." She stared down at her coffee cup.

"And my coming back early messed everything

up for you. You were planning on staying here while going to school, weren't you?"

"Don't worry about it, Matt. Life happens."

Matt nearly groaned aloud. *Life happens!* He could still hear his mother telling him those same words when he was twelve and she was yanking him from yet another school to go to yet another town. *"Listen, Matthew Michael Stone, life happens. Get over it and adjust or you will never survive in this world."* He didn't believe life just happened. A person could control his own destiny if he chose. Matt had chosen his destiny the day he graduated from high school and told his mother he was tired of searching for answers when he had never known the questions. He was going to go to college, get a job, and settle down in one place. She was more than welcome to visit him whenever she was in his part of the country. At last report, Veronica Stone was still searching for her answers, living in some New Age community outside of Phoenix, Arizona, worshiping compost and selling crystals to stressed-out Baby Boomers who were looking for inner peace.

Beulah Crawford obviously had the same outlook on life as his mother and he would be well advised to see her to the door immediately. But the dejected slump of her shoulders ricocheted the guilt back onto him. He had come home early and ruined her plans.

She pushed her chair back. "Well, I guess I'll go pack."

"No, wait." The thought of her leaving caused him to break out in a sweat. If she left now, how could he forgive himself? Swallowing the last of his milk, Matt visualized what her bedroom looked like when he'd peeked in while she was showering. Clothes were scattered over the furniture, shoes lay about, and a pile of books balanced precariously on the nightstand. He knew what she was facing while reaching for her dream. He had faced the same walls, the same mountains that had to be climbed. He could no more turn her away than stop feeding his cats. Something about Blue intrigued him. Something besides her stunning body and beautiful face. Beulah Crawford was the worst possible woman for him, and he would be a wiser man if he kept remembering that. "Blue, I have an idea."

"About what?"

"You have to spend the night at least. It's too late now to drive down the mountain and get a room. Besides, there are two bedrooms here."

She drummed her fingers against her still-full coffee cup. "Okay, Matt, I'll stay the night. Thank you."

Matt suppressed his smile. It had taken her exactly sixty-two seconds to deem him safe enough to spend the night with. He had counted every second. "I want you to sleep on the idea I have in mind. You can give me your answer in the morning. It might take weeks, if not longer, for you to find another housesitting job in this area. As you can see, I'm at a disadvantage here." He nodded at the crutches leaning against the table. "I can't drive for at least three weeks, perhaps longer, and I live pretty far from town. Why don't you stay here, there's plenty of room. You can help around the house and keep up the domestic end."

"Keep up the domestic end?" She started to chuckle, then halted. "Are you serious?"

"Sure, why not?" When she stared dubiously at him, he continued. "Listen, Blue, you don't have to do it. I just thought it could solve both our problems. If you don't do it, I'll have to hire someone to drive me to the doctors, to do my food shopping, and all those other little jobs that must be done. Why don't you think on it tonight like I suggested? I'm really bushed. I've crossed so many time zones today that my body thinks it's next week. Can you feed the cats and lock up for the night?"

Matt slowly rose to his feet, trying to mask the pain the simple movement caused. After carefully positioning the crutches, he said, "Good night, Blue."

Blue watched him make his way out of the kitchen and whispered, "Good night, Matt." The poor man. He was in such pain and he needed her. It would be the perfect solution to her dilemma. She could stay here free, keep her part-time job, attend classes, and take care of Matt. How much trouble could one healthy man on crutches be? For ten grueling and dispiriting years she had taken care of her father while his health gave out on him. Matt

Stone would be a piece of cake compared with the disagreeable and nasty-tempered Neville Crawford.

Blue loaded the dishwasher and fed the cats. All the while she counted her lucky stars and the money Matt was going to save her.

TWO

An hour later Blue stared at the bedroom ceiling and rationalized her decision for the fourth time. Her savings were minimal. The sale of her father's Iowa farm two years earlier should had netted her enough profit to put herself through college if she were careful. No one had ever called Beulah Crawford careful. She led with her heart and prayed that the guts she'd inherited from her mother would be enough to see her through. The person who had wanted to buy the farm, because it adjoined his own, was the person who could afford it the least, Caleb Willing. Caleb was two years older than she, her nearest neighbor, and when they were adolescents with hormones ruling their heads, he was the boy who had taught her to kiss. Luckily his head had been clearer than hers, or they would have done more than just kiss. During the years she took care of her father, Caleb had always been there for her.

So when her father had passed away and she was free to leave, she'd wanted Caleb to buy the farm. They had worked it out with a lawyer, and the property had been placed in Caleb's name with the condition that he'd make small quarterly payments to her for the next twenty years.

Blue considered herself lucky. She had come into this world naked, crying, and without a penny to her name. She now had two duffel bags filled with clothes, a ten-by-ten rental unit back in Iowa crammed with family heirlooms, a motorcycle, and quarterly checks that covered a portion of her college tuition. She had more than most people. She also had a dream. A dream that was within her grasp, if she could just hold it all together till May.

If she earned free room and board helping out Matt, then the little she made working down at Jack's Diner would cover the cost of books, supplies, and quite possibly a car. She needed something to drive around during the winter months. Matt would need his Bronco, and her motorcycle would be suicidal on icy mountain roads. If she pinched every gram of copper out of every penny, she might have enough to rent a cheap apartment next semester and still graduate come May. It was possible. So the financial end of the decision looked positive.

The physical end, on the other hand, definitely looked shaky. Could she possibly stay in the same house with Matt Stone for a few months without making a fool of herself by jumping his bones? And what great bones they were! Computer nerds be damned. If she'd known keyboard jocks looked like Matt, she would have enrolled in some computer courses.

During her eight-week stay at Matt's home, she had discovered a great deal about the man. He was single and he wasn't the world's swingingest bachelor. No mirrors graced his bedroom ceiling. No whirlpool tub, built for two, adorned his bathroom. No forgotten articles of female clothing were stashed in his closet. Hell, his nightstand didn't even contain a packet of condoms. She had known it was morally wrong to go snooping through drawers and closets, but after a couple of weeks curiosity had gotten the better of her. What if she had found evidence that he was a serial killer? What if she had started to receive strange phone calls or visitors? She had reasoned with herself that she needed to know more about the mysterious Matthew Stone.

Problem was, the more she discovered, the more fascinated she'd become. He was neat, possibly to the point of obsessiveness. The entire house had been spotless when she arrived. Cans of vegetables and soups had been neatly stacked in cabinets, with all the labels facing front. Every glass and plate in the kitchen matched. The magazines had been current and placed precisely in the rack. Even the pillows on the couch had been positioned perfectly. It had been freaky to live in the house during the first week or so. Eventually her own method of housekeeping had replaced Matt's.

The house was decorated in quiet colors that spoke of good taste with money to match. Even the back den, where Matt kept an army of computers, was color-coordinated and immaculate. There were no frilly knickknacks, personal pictures, or unwanted clutter anywhere, except in the guest bedroom. Her bedroom. She immediately picked the guest bedroom over the sterile-looking master bedroom when she moved into the house. There was something "homey" about the room. Something safe and comfortable.

The walls were painted a light cream, the carpet was beige, and the furniture was pine, all of which matched the rest of the house perfectly. What made the room different was that Matt had hung sheer white curtains at the huge window overlooking the forest and lined the top of the dresser with half a dozen plants. Six original pieces of art decorated the walls, and the quilt on the double-size bed was such a multitude of bright colors that she had fallen in love with it on sight.

The built-in bookcase, next to the closet, was crammed with the most unusual assortment of souvenirs. She had spent hours examining the different pieces and marveling at the museum, town, or attraction each had been acquired from. Was there really a Frederick's Bra Museum in Hollywood, California? Or a place called Toilet Rock in City of Rocks, New Mexico? The Spongeorama in Tarpon Springs, Florida, was beyond belief. Who ever heard of an entire place dedicated to sponges?

Had Matt really visited all these places? Or did the souvenirs have something to do with the only photograph in the entire house? In a silver frame, positioned on the nightstand next to the bed, was a picture of a woman. It was hard to tell the woman's age, but Blue placed her between forty-five and fifty. She was standing outside, with dry harsh-looking mountains in the background. Blue placed it somewhere in the Southwest, if not another country altogether. The woman was wearing a yellow top, a billowing calf-length skirt, and Indian moccasins. Her hair was braided into a thick rope that reached her waist. She also was wearing half a dozen necklaces, four earrings that Blue could count, and the most beautiful smile. Blue had no idea who the woman was, but she knew instantly that she would like her and that, for some reason, this room felt like hers.

Now that she had met Matt, she could see a family resemblance. The woman was either an older sister or his mother. Blue smiled into the dark. Imagine, Matt having that woman for a mother! It was inconceivable. The woman appeared to be dainty and bubbling over with excitement, even standing still. Matt was over six feet tall, with shoulders that could block out those mountains in the background, and had a reserved manner about him.

Blue kicked off the sheet as her temperature rose a couple of degrees, owing nothing to the heat outside. With a muffled curse, she rolled over and punched the pillow. She willed herself to think of something other than Matt's body. What did it matter how broad his shoulders were? She needed to concentrate on his behavior if she was staying.

He had peeked while she was getting out of the pool. She would bet her life on that, but he had not revealed his treachery by word or deed. She had expected some comment, but he had been the perfect gentleman. In fact, he had purposely mentioned the house's two bedrooms. Was that to put her mind at ease, or his own?

Blue smiled as she remembered that Matt wanted her to help out around the house. While other girls back home had entered the pie-baking contests, Blue had always won the "Catch the Greased Pig" contest. Other girls bought dresses and makeup and went on dates. Blue wore jeans, baseball caps, and had come home with a trophy in the local motocross bike race just to show her father she wasn't about to conform to his idea of a woman.

She did not race motorcycles anymore, but she still rode one. *Blue's Lightning* had been with her since she was sixteen and won her first trophy. She would rather have all her hair fall out before she would even think about getting rid of it. Her father had forbidden her to ride "Satan's device," as he referred to it. Blue had hidden it in Caleb's barn and had ridden it behind her father's back. Just like everything else she had done the first twenty-seven years of her life. Neville Crawford had approved of nothing, and had allowed nothing in regard to her life.

Her mother, Mary, had died when Blue was ten, after a short battle with cancer. Her father, who had been a happy and loving man, had changed on the day they lowered her mother's casket into the spring-softened ground. He'd always been a religious man, but his wife's death changed his views on God and sin, heaven and hell. Instead of raving against God for taking his beloved wife, he accused Mary of sins she didn't commit. Her death, he said, was her punishment. Neville devoted his life thereafter to ensuring that Blue committed no sins.

Blue had been a dutiful daughter until the end. And while she had regrets, they weren't as many as she would have had if she had gotten on *Blue's Lightning* and ridden away from their Iowa farm, leaving her father to the neighbors, the church, and more than likely the state.

Now she had another man who needed her. But this time it was different. A smile touched her lips as she drifted off to sleep, secure in the knowledge that Matt only needed her legs, her ability to drive, and her help around the house. He didn't need her heart, her soul, or her life.

Matt stared at his bedroom ceiling and thought about Blue sleeping in the bed in the next room. Whatever in the world had possessed him to invite her to stay? She was the worst possible candidate for a housekeeper. She couldn't make a decent cup of coffee. Judging from the condition of his bedroom and the rest of the house, he would say she never met a dust rag. Hell, she couldn't even manage to scramble up some eggs. He was either going to starve to death or be buried under dust.

It had to be jet lag. What other possible explanation could there be?

Matt was careful not to jar his right thigh as he rolled over and pictured Blue as she had stood naked in the darkness. She was a golden goddess with a body to tempt the strongest mortal. He really should not have looked, it was not the gentlemanly thing to do. Now he was paying the price. He kicked off the sheet with his left leg. The rising heat in the bedroom had nothing to do with the temperature outside.

He squeezed his eyes shut and started to count sheep. Soft fuzzy sheep that for some strange reason had sky-blue eyes and a dusting of freckles across their noses. Their gentle baas lulled him to sleep.

Blue stood in the kitchen humming, trying to decipher the instructions on the box of instant pancake mix. When she heard Matt on the stairs, she ran nervous fingers through her hair and eyed the coffeemaker. It had taken her three tries to finally make a pot fit to drink.

Sunshine streamed in the windows, causing Matt to squint as he hobbled into the room. He looked like a little boy who had just stumbled from his bed, she thought with amusement. Putting on a bright, cheerful smile, she used her best "house-keeper" voice and said, "Good morning, Matt."

He gripped his crutches so tightly his knuckles turned white. After a mumbled good morning, he made his way to the table.

Blue poured Matt's coffee. He was definitely not a morning person. Maybe the coffee would wake him up. She placed the cup before him and stretched her smile. "Sleep well?"

His own smile looked forced. "I slept like a baby."

"Would you like some pancakes?"

He glanced cautiously at the counter, then back at her. "Sure, just one or two, though. I'm not a big breakfast eater."

He watched as she pulled out bowls, measuring cups, and a frying pan. "Does all this mean you're staying?"

"If you're sure you want to chance my cooking."

He nodded at the paraphernalia on the counter. "Has it killed anyone yet?"

She chuckled. He didn't seem too concerned about the prospect, even though her father, on more than one occasion, had accused her of trying to poison him. "Not that I'm aware of."

He took a tentative sip of coffee. "Hey, the coffee's pretty good this morning."

Her chest puffed out with pride. "Thank you." She concentrated on beating the batter with a fork. The package said to mix just until the large lumps disappeared and to leave the small ones. She wondered what constituted a small lump. Under one inch? Shrugging, she poured some of the thick gooey batter into the hot frying pan. "What time do you usually have breakfast?"

"I'm normally an early riser. I slept late this morning because of the time change."

She glanced at the clock. It was seven-thirty. With a silent groan she went back to the two bubbling pancakes, which somehow took up the whole pan. After flipping them, she took out a plate and placed the bottle of syrup on the table.

"How's your leg this morning?" she asked as she proudly set the plate containing the pancakes in front of him.

He stared at the pancakes, then poured a small river of syrup over them before answering. "Stiff and sore. I guess that's to be expected after all the traveling yesterday. Later on this morning I'll go soak it in the pool, if that's okay with you?"

"Sure. It's your pool, Matt. I won't even be here."

The first mouthful of pancakes halted in midair. "You won't?"

"Oh, I forgot to tell you last night. I have a part-time job down at Jack's Diner. Jack's agreed to work around my class schedule once school starts tomorrow." She pulled out a chair and sat across from him. "You won't be needing me here twenty-four hours a day, will you?" She hadn't thought about that. Maybe Matt expected her to be at his beck and call all day. If that was the case, she couldn't accept the free room and board. Classes started tomorrow, and the job at Jack's would help pay for the car she needed.

"No, I can manage pretty well on my own. I'll schedule my doctor's appointments and anything else I might be needing you for, for when you're available."

She watched as he ate the forkful of pancakes and chewed, and chewed, and chewed. Desperately attempting to distract him, she said, "I'll get you a copy of my class schedule. If you could work around that, it would be great. Jack's pretty decent about my hours. He prefers me to work the early-morning shift, or the late shift."

Matt frowned at his plate as he swallowed. "What do you do, waitress?" He speared two more pieces and ran them through the stream of syrup.

She almost told him no, that she was the cook, but she didn't think Matt was in the mood. He appeared to be suffering through her pancakes and she didn't want to torture the poor man any more than necessary. She couldn't figure out how those large bubbles had gotten cooked into the pancakes. The golden-brown pancakes looked fluffy and light, except for those huge bubbles, which gave them the appearance of the moon's surface.

"Yes, I'm a waitress," she finally said. "The younger waitresses don't like to get up at four A.M. or work the late shift, which would put a crimp in their hot dates."

Matt popped another bite of pancake into his mouth and chewed and chewed.

Blue silently groaned as he started to choke. He used a mouthful of coffee to wash down whatever had been caught in his throat. Maybe one of the bubbles had gotten lodged in his windpipe. Lord, she didn't know if she could remember her CPR.

He looked up at her. "You don't have any hot dates?"

She chuckled. "Girls who grew up in Cobs Corner, Iowa, don't go out on hot dates."

"Why not?" He pushed his half-full plate away. "If they all look as cute as you, I'm sure Cobs Corner was one hopping place."

With a disgusted gesture, she swiped at the freckles dusting her nose. "Thanks, I think." Cute was not the image she wanted to project to Matt or any other male.

She placed her empty coffee cup in the dishwasher. "I have to go to the campus and pick up my books, then I'm working the lunch shift at Jack's. I should be back around three. Do you need me to pick up anything in town?"

"No, thank you. I have everything I need."

"What about dinner? Anything in particular that you want or like?"

"We can discuss dinner when you get home."

She opened up her dark green backpack and searched for paper and a pen. "What kind of food do you like and what do you hate?" she asked as she pulled out a note pad and a pen. Being his housekeeper meant she had to at least attempt to prepare meals that he liked. And do his laundry. And she really should take a vacuum and dust rag to the living room. And then there were the bathrooms, and what about his den? Did one dust computers or just blow the dust off? Cripes, this housekeeper bit was going to turn into a full-time job if she wasn't careful.

She glanced up and mustered a small smile. "Are you allergic to anything?"

"No." He glanced at his half-eaten pancakes. "I basically eat just about anything. Except liver or spinach."

She raised an eyebrow. "Popeye would disapprove."

"Popeye dated a woman named after salad dressing."

She chuckled, but dutifully wrote: *No liver, No spinach*. Directly underneath she wrote: *Scrub toilets* and *Do laundry*. "Anything else I should note?"

"Not that I can think of, Blue. If you have time, can you stop at the post office and pick up my mail?"

"Sure. I just sent a stack of your mail about three days ago. But you've gotten a couple more letters that look important since then, and they're on the desk in the den. And then there's the box of junk mail I've been accumulating."

"You've been saving my junk mail?"

"Well, one man's junk is another man's treasure, and I didn't want to be responsible for ditching your treasures, so I found a box to put them in. It's in the den too."

"Sounds like my work for the morning is cut out for me."

"You should rest that leg." She noticed how he had his right leg propped up on a chair.

"Don't worry. I think it's impossible to strain it by opening letters."

She closed the notepad and replaced it in her backpack. "Well, if you're sure you're going to be all right here alone, I guess I'll be going now."

"I'll be fine." He watched as she opened the hall closet and pulled out her denim jacket and motorcycle helmet. "What's that?"

"It's a motorcycle helmet. What does it look like?"

"You drive a motorcycle?"

Blue shifted her weight and stared at Matt. There was an undertone of something in his voice. She didn't know what, but it put her on edge. All her life she had heard it from her father, until she had hidden the cycle in Caleb's barn. She wasn't about to hide it again. "I've driven one since I was twelve, Matt."

"You can borrow my Bronco. I won't be needing it."

Now she heard a patronizing tone in his voice. Was it because he thought she couldn't handle a bike? Or was it because she was a woman? Or maybe he was like her father and just hated motorcycles. "No, thank you." She tried to keep her own voice neutral and pleasant, but it was a strain. "I'm perfectly capable of driving a motorcycle."

"I'm sure you can handle a cycle, Blue. It's the other drivers I'm worried about."

"I'm a big girl, Matt. I know the dangers of riding a motorcycle. I just happen to think those dangers are outweighed by the joys of having the wind blowing in my face and the road roaring beneath my feet. If being your housekeeper means you're going to dictate the vehicle I drive, I don't think this arrangement will work out."

"You're right. If you want to drive a motorcycle, go ahead. But the Bronco is free if you want to borrow it. I won't be able to drive it for weeks." He eyed the crutches leaning against the table. "I would appreciate it if you use it once in a while to keep it running." He reached for the crutches and hauled himself out of the chair.

"No problem," she said. "I'm going to need it to get you into town for your doctor visits anyway, and cycles weren't built for food shopping." She pulled on her jacket and headed for the door. "If you call your doctor this morning, see if tomorrow late afternoon or evening is okay for an appointment. I only have morning classes tomorrow."

He followed her into the living room. "I'll see if they can get me in then."

"Great." She opened the door and stepped out onto the porch. "I wrote Jack's Diner's phone number next to the phone in the kitchen in case you need to get in touch with me."

"I'll be fine. Go to work, Blue." He leaned against the doorjamb and watched as she walked toward the garage.

The clock read three-ten when Matt finally heard Blue's motorcycle coming up the drive. He stepped back from the screen door as she came into view. He did not want her to know he'd been waiting for her. That morning when she'd rolled her motorcycle out of his garage, he had breathed a sigh of relief. The 350 Honda wasn't as big as he had feared. It looked like a nice reasonable bike for her to drive. Still, the thought of some other driver plowing into her had worried him.

The day had dragged on forever, three o'clock never seeming to come. Now that it was here and she had returned safe and sound, he was still uncertain how to handle the situation. He had absolutely no right to forbid her to ride the bike.

After she had left that morning, he'd cleaned up the kitchen and thrown away the remainder of his pancakes. They hadn't been that bad. They hadn't been that good either, but they had been edible. They had certainly been an improvement over the scrambled eggs.

He'd spent the rest of the day going through the mail, exercising in the pool, and resting. Around two he had thawed a small roast—one he had frozen before leaving for Germany, and which Blue would probably never have cooked—and put it in the oven with some potatoes, but no carrots. The cupboards were pretty bare, if not downright empty. He would write out a grocery list and pray Blue's aversion to cooking didn't go as far as food shopping. He didn't relish the idea of hobbling up and down aisles on crutches while pushing a cart. A person had to eat, and Blue had accepted the position of temporary housekeeper and chauffeur.

He sat down on the couch a moment before she walked into the house. Her backpack was bulging, no doubt filled with newly purchased books, and she looked tired and windblown. "Hi," he said. "Have a good day?" It was an inane way of greeting someone, but he was at a loss for words. He'd never had to welcome somebody home before, especially when it was his home.

She dropped the pack on the floor and tossed her jacket and helmet onto a chair. With a weary sigh she fell onto the sofa and closed her eyes.

"That bad?" With her eyes closed, he took the chance to openly examine her body and face. Last night's vision hadn't been a fluke or a trick of light. Blue was small, compact, and gorgeous.

She opened her eyes. He hadn't noticed before how her blue eyes seemed to sparkle with some hidden mirth. "Lord, I feel old compared to most of the students. Hell, all of the students." She sighed. "Where do they get all that energy?"

"You don't look old." Actually, he thought she looked great, but he supposed that wasn't the kind of statement one made to one's housekeeper.

She arched a golden eyebrow. "Thanks, I think." She wiggled her butt into a more comfortable position. "Maybe this living together won't be so bad after all."

"Are you having doubts?"

"Not really. I think it will take some adjustments on both our parts, but it's feasible."

He didn't like the sound of this. "What kind of adjustments?"

"Scheduling our moonlight swims so we can avoid any more embarrassing moments."

"Point taken." He tried to cover his chuckle with a fake cough. "Anything else?"

"I heard that laugh, Stone."

She gave him a look that clearly was meant to be intimidating, but failed. Blue couldn't be intimidating with an entire army at her back. Now, put a frying pan in her hand . . .

She went on. "You don't see me laughing over your obsession with collecting cheap and gaudy souvenirs, do you?"

He grinned. He liked her honesty. Not too many people would have called the collection of souvenirs in the guest bedroom cheap and gaudy, even though that was what they were. Most people would refer to them as unusual or unique, or at least interesting. Not Blue, though. She called things as she saw them. His mother would love her.

Matt abruptly stood up, using the arm of the couch for leverage. His traitorous thoughts had no right heading in that direction. It didn't matter what his mother would think of Blue. The idea of his mother liking her should have him running in the opposite direction. So why wasn't he? He glanced over at Blue, still lying on the couch, and smiled. She didn't look like any housekeeper he'd ever envisioned.

She frowned up at him and sniffed. "What is that I smell?"

"Pot roast."

"But I'm supposed to do the cooking, remember?"

With what he hoped was an innocent smile, he started back toward the kitchen. "I know, but I got bored all by myself. There wasn't anything to do."

Blue groaned as she rose from the couch and followed him into the sunny yellow kitchen. She peeked into the stove. "It looks delicious, Matt. How long do I have before dinner?"

"Time enough for a quick dip in the pool."

"You'll join me?"

He nervously rubbed his right thigh and thought about the red and swollen nine-inch scar that would be visible if he wore a bathing suit. "Not right now. Maybe later on tonight."

Her gaze had followed the movement of his hand, but she made no comment. "I think I'll just take a quick shower," she said, "and wash the smell of french fries and onions off me. It's one of the disadvantages of working in a diner. You end up smelling like food all day."

He leaned in closer and sniffed her neck. "Is

that what I've been smelling?" His nose wrinkled. "I thought it was some new perfume designed to drive men crazy." He saw the pulse at the base of her throat quicken. His heartbeat matched hers as desire flooded his body. He wanted to press his lips to that pounding pulse.

He slowly raised his gaze to her eyes. She felt it too! He could see it in the darkening of her eyes. The air between them became charged with the electricity of their attraction. All he had to do was lean five inches closer.

His voice deepened with anticipation. "You smell good enough to eat."

Her gaze seemed riveted to his mouth. "I do?"

He watched as her pink tongue swept across her lower lip, leaving a moist sheen. It was all the invitation he needed. He took a step closer, then howled in pain as he forgot about his injured leg and had placed all his weight upon it. He hissed air in between his teeth and blinked away the stars that had appeared in his eyes.

Blue backed away. "Matt, are you all right? Is there anything I can do?" She glanced from his leg, to the crutches, to his clenched jaw.

The pain subsided to the point where he could at least answer her. "It's fine now, Blue." He felt like a complete ass. How could he have been so caught up in the moment as to forget about his leg? *Real smooth, Stone!* "I think I'll go prop it up until dinner is ready." He couldn't even bring himself to face her as he hobbled from the kitchen.

THREE

With a groan Matt rolled over and glared at the clock on the nightstand. It was after eight. He had missed Blue. She had left hours ago for the diner, to work the breakfast shift, and then she had classes till two. How could he have overslept? Simple. After hearing Blue retire to her room the night before, he hadn't been able to sleep. Visions of Blue had kept him up, in more ways than one. He had ended up doing countless laps in the cool pool, then tossing and turning into the small hours of morning.

He grabbed a crutch and headed for a cold shower. Life before Blue had been so much easier. He'd never had to confront one particular dark side of his personality—lust.

Twenty minutes later he made his way down the stairs and into the kitchen. He smiled when he saw the table. It was set for one, complete with place mat, bowl, spoon, and a box of Corn Flakes. Placed in the center of the table was a vase filled with wild-flowers, and propped against it was a note addressed to him.

You seemed to be sleeping like a baby, he read, *so I didn't want to wake you. I'll be home about four. I borrowed your Bronco so I can food-shop and pick up a pizza for dinner. Remember your doctor's appointment is at seven. Blue.* So, he mused, it looked like he didn't have to worry about Blue driving her motorcycle that day, what she might cook for dinner, or if she was upset about the kiss that had almost happened in the kitchen. Pizza was totally harmless and the note could have been written by his mother.

He groaned with embarrassment as he realized Blue must have checked in on him that morning. Although he was no prude, he wasn't used to being checked out while he slept. Especially since he didn't own any pajamas.

At half-past ten Matt was working at his desk when a loud pounding interrupted him. Someone was beating on his front door. Muttering curses, he hobbled to the door and flung it open, then glared at his friend Jared Miller, who was standing on the porch. "Good morning, Jared. You can wipe that silly smirk off your face."

Jared chuckled and entered the living room. "Now, why would I be smirking?" He glanced at the crutches and his smile faded.

"Let me see," Matt said. "When we talked on the phone when I first got to Germany, you said something along the lines of, 'Don't worry about the house or cats. I've met your housesitter and she seems perfect. I ran a police check on her anyway, and she's clean as a whistle. She reminds me of Alison's aunt Clarrisa.'" With an exasperated sigh, Matt lowered himself onto the couch. "Which reminds me, who in the hell is Aunt Clarrisa?"

Jared made himself at home in Matt's recliner. "She's the black sheep of Alison's family." He grabbed a handful of M&M's from the candy dish sitting on the nearby table. "She was a flower child in the sixties and went to Berkeley and got a degree in something or another. After graduation she moved to a commune to meditate and become one with Mother Nature. She left the commune some years back with her daughter, Sky. At last report she was making and selling chainsaw sculptures. I only met her once a couple of years ago."

"Blue reminds you of her?" Matt asked, incredulous. Good Lord, what had happened to Jared's mind while he was away?

"It's the eyes. They have the same laughing eyes."

Matt ran a hand through his hair. "You tell me my housesitter's perfect because she has the same kind of eyes as your wife's crazy aunt."

Jared reached for another handful of candy. "Don't call Alison's aunt crazy. My wife happens to be very fond of Clarrisa."

"That's your problem, Jared, not mine."

Jared's eyebrows rose. "You don't like Blue?"

Matt looked away from his friend and studied

the candy dish Blue had placed on the table. He wondered why he had never thought to put one out. Shaking his head to chase away a golden ghost with tangled curls and an extremely kissable mouth, he answered, "Of course I like her."

Jared's eyebrows arched higher. "So what's the problem?"

"Who said there was a problem?" There were a thousand problems, but he'd be damned before he'd admit that to Jared.

"Matt, are you on pain pills?" Jared leaned forward and tried to study Matt's eyes.

"No. Why would I take painkillers if there isn't any pain?" That wasn't entirely true. When he had placed all his weight on the leg the night before, he'd felt the agonizing pain of his muscle screaming in protest. But if he was careful he didn't need the medication the doctors had prescribed.

Jared reached for another fistful of M&M's as he rose from the chair. "Listen, buddy, take it easy for a while. I saw Blue at Jack's this morning and she told me about your accident. Since I was in the area I stopped by to make sure you were okay. Give me or Alison a call if you need anything."

Matt watched as Jared headed for the door. "Thanks, but I hired Blue as my housekeeper and chauffeur until I'm back on my feet."

Jared grinned knowingly. "Smart move, buddy."

"What the hell is that supposed to mean?" He didn't need Jared or anyone else in town getting the wrong idea about himself and Blue. It was bad enough his body already had the wrong idea.

Jared held up one hand in a gesture of peace. "It doesn't mean anything." He popped an M&M into his mouth and winked. "She does set a mean candy dish, though." Opening the door, he stepped out onto the wooden porch, then looked back at Matt. "There is one thing I'm curious about."

"What's that?"

"Where are all the yellow M&M's?"

Jared closed the door, and Matt looked at the candy dish. Jared was right. There wasn't a yellow piece of candy in the bowl.

It was past two before Matt completed his laps in the pool. He gingerly pulled himself out of the water and with the aid of his crutches made it to the lounge chair. He settled into it with a groan, grateful for the warming rays of the sun. The specialist in Germany was right; swimming was therapeutic. Today he'd managed two more laps than yesterday, and he was able to put a little more weight on his leg. Confident that his recovery was on schedule, he let his thoughts drift to a more enticing subject—Blue.

What was so different about this woman? What attracted him so? She was all wrong for him. Candy dishes, bunny slippers, and mornings when he could sleep in were completely foreign to him. His life ran like a precision clock, with his work and play time calculated to the second. Ever since he was a small boy he had known what and where he wanted to be. Now he had reached his goals, and there was no room for dreamers like Blue. She was a searcher, just like his mother. Blue went from housesitting assignment to housesitting assignment, doing "a little of this and a little of that," while piecing together a college education. She was looking for something, that elusive pot of gold at the end of every rainbow. Always running from life, while claiming to be searching for it.

He, on the other hand, had found the life he wanted. His business was secure and he was well-off. He'd bought himself a nice slice of Mother Nature and built this house. For the first time in his life he had roots. It had been hard work, but it was worth every ounce of sweat, every hour of lost sleep, and all those years of dreaming. There would be no more running to or from anything.

The warmth of the sun lured him into a light slumber, and contrary to his new resolve to ignore Blue, he dreamed of a mermaid with golden hair and laughing blue eyes who tried to entice him into searching the deep blue sea for sunken treasure.

Blue's precarious grip on two overstuffed shopping bags slipped as she inserted her key into the lock. As the front door swung open five apples and two cans of soup rolled across the porch. Sighing, she stepped over the roving fruit and headed for the kitchen. Depositing the bags on the counter, she called Matt's name.

Silence.

She headed upstairs. "Matt," she called softly before knocking and opening his bedroom door. The room was empty and the bed neatly made. Where could he be? She walked over to the window and looked down. A soft smile touched her lips. Matt was sleeping by the pool. She headed back downstairs and to the Bronco for the pizza and the last bag of groceries.

After putting away the food, Blue changed into her bathing suit and joined Matt on the deck. When she'd peeked in on him that morning, she had seen only his bare back. A dark blue cotton sheet had been draped low on his hips. This afternoon she had a full frontal view of his gorgeous body, except for where a pair of hunter-green swim trunks barely covered his essentials. And what impressive-looking essentials they were.

For being such a large man, she was amazed not to see an extra ounce of fat anywhere. Muscles bulged in a broad tanned chest covered with fine chestnut-colored curls. His stomach was flat and smooth. A scattering of soft downy hair disappeared into the low-riding waistband of his suit. Blue sighed wishfully and dragged her gaze past the green suit to his scar.

The swollen red scar ran down the outside of his mid-thigh and was about nine inches long. She could still see where the stitches had been. It looked like he would always have a scar. She lifted her gaze back to his face. He didn't look like he was in any pain, so maybe the leg was healing. There were no other visible scars.

Matt stirred in his sleep. She quickly turned and dived into the pool before he awoke and caught her drooling over him like some schoolgirl. Between catching him unaware today and the tan line she had observed that morning, she realized Matt usually swam with a suit on. So the first night they met was an exception for them both. She had never gone skinny-dipping before then.

When she reached the deep end, she flipped over and floated on her back and thought of Matt. Since he didn't call out to her, he still must be sleeping. Matt, she decided, must sleep like the dead.

Matt had been jerked awake by the sound of splashing. Blue must be home, was his first thought. Without moving a muscle, he peeked out from under his lashes and watched her swim the length of the pool. He got his first look at her bathing suit when she turned onto her back to float. It was a one-piece, turquoise, and the V plunged almost to her navel. He silently cursed his body's reaction as desire shot through his groin. He sat up and raised the back of the recliner, hoping to hide his obvious response to her.

She apparently heard him, for she called out, "Good afternoon, sleepyhead."

"You're home early."

She dropped her legs down and treaded water, sending him an amused look. "It's about four-thirty."

He watched as she swam to the shallow end. Soft womanly shoulders emerged from the sparkling water. He held his breath as rounded breasts followed. She leisurely climbed the steps from the pool, and he watched as she reached up and squeezed the excess water from her hair. She shook her head, and curls sprang in every direction. His worst fears were realized as his gaze traveled down her body. The bottom of the suit was cut up to her hips, revealing the entire length of her smooth tanned legs, ending in delicate ankles. Fastened around her right ankle was a gold bracelet. He stared fascinated at the glittering gold as Blue walked over to a chair and reached for her towel.

With a violent thrust Matt released the back of his chair and flipped over onto his stomach.

"Matt? Are you all right?"

He sucked a lungful of air and wondered how he was going to speak. "It's nothing, just a twinge." His voice was husky and raw. He buried his face in his arms and muttered a comment on what exactly was twinging.

"Can I get you something for the pain?" she asked, sounding concerned.

Visions of her helping to relieve his pain only increased the pressure. Moaning silently, Matt forced himself to concentrate on Einstein's theory of relativity. Feeling more in control, he said, "I don't believe in pain pills." Besides, he didn't know of any pills you could buy over the counter to help with his problem.

She said nothing more as she finished drying off and sat down in the chair next to him.

"Did you get the pizza?" he asked, turning his head to look at her.

"Yes, I put it in the refrigerator. As soon as you're ready for dinner all I'll have to do is nuke it."

He chuckled. "Somehow it doesn't seem very appetizing when you refer to it as nuking."

"Sorry." After a moment she said, "I got half with pepperoni and half with extra cheese. Is that okay?"

"Sure. I told you I eat just about anything."

"Tomorrow I have classes till four. I'll cook up a better dinner than nuked pizza. Chicken should be easy to make."

The way she said it made his stomach roll. With the instinct of a desperate man, he injected some hurt into his voice. "I was planning on going out for dinner. I haven't been out for a good meal in weeks. Believe me, hospital food is the pits." He put on his best hangdog expression and added, "Especially foreign hospital food."

"Okay, if you want to go out, go. I'll cook you a decent meal some other time."

He hesitated, then said, "I was hoping you'd join me."

"Me?"

Matt saw her smile and knew he was in trouble.

Here he was staring at Blue's lips and tasting them in his mind. Honey. Pure sweet honey. They would respond so innocently to his bidding. As heat assaulted his body and his breath quickened, he silently berated himself. Why was it every time Blue came within ten feet of him, his hormones stood at attention, all in a very obvious place? Mad at himself for asking, at his body for lusting, and at Blue for just being Blue, he said, "Sure, why not? Someone has to drive the Bronco."

Her smile turned empty and the laughter in her eyes faded. "Okay." She stood and picked up her towel. "Let me know when you want the Bronco ready."

Before Matt could wipe the astonished look from his face, she was walking toward the house. She called over her shoulder that dinner would be ready in fifteen minutes. With a muffled curse he reached for his crutches and hoisted himself from the lounge chair. He made his way to the edge of the pool, dropped the crutches on the deck, and fell face-first into the cool water, yelling "Women!"

A spitting and sputtering Matt surfaced with one very important lesson learned. When you fall into a pool face-first, close your mouth. He glared at the house and wondered what had happened. After replaying the conversation in his mind, he realized why Blue's mood had changed. He'd mentioned needing a driver, not a date. Great, now he'd insulted her.

How could one woman cause so many problems? He pulled himself out of the pool, reached for his crutches, and headed after Blue.

Her bedroom door was closed, and he knocked on it with a hint of impatience.

"What?" came the muffled response.

"Are you decent?"

"As decent as I get," she answered.

Matt took a deep breath and opened the door. She was standing at the bureau brushing her damp hair, wearing faded cutoffs and a baggy T-shirt with Donald Duck's picture on it.

When he just stood there watching her, she snapped, "Can I get you something?"

"I would like you to have dinner with me tomorrow night."

With a slight tilt of her head she said, "I already said I would take you."

"No, Blue." He hobbled into the room until he was only an arm's length from her. "I mean would you go to dinner with me, as in a date?"

"Date?"

"Yes." What could one date hurt? he asked himself. Surely it would just enforce what he already knew; they were totally opposite from each other. Contrary to what romantics said, opposites did not attract. Balancing on his crutches, he reached out and traced her lower lip with the tip of his finger. Well, they didn't attract much. "Will you?"

Her voice was breathless and low. "Yes."

"Do you mind driving?"

"Of course not."

He smiled and dropped his hand. "Good." He wanted to kiss her, to taste her, but he remembered last night's painful lesson. He didn't relish making a fool out of himself two nights in a row. He backed away toward the door. "I'll be down in about ten minutes. See you then."

He left her room and headed for a cold shower. What was she doing to him? All she had to do was look at him and he wanted her. He never should have asked her to stay. The heat between them was too powerful. Too tempting.

Blue glanced at the artful display behind the plate-glass window. She was at the right place—Martha's Thrift Shop. She shifted her helmet to her other hand and pushed open the door. Two elderly saleswomen turned and smiled. Blue swallowed hard. How was she going to explain to these two innocent-looking ladies that she wanted a dress that would knock Matt off his crutches? She wanted Matt to kiss her. Twice now she had seen the desire flare in his eyes, but he hadn't acted on it. Why? Was it because she was his housekeeper? Tonight she wanted to show him she wasn't just a housekeeper and chauffeur. She wanted those kisses his eyes kept promising.

"Good morning," the ladies said in unison.

"Ah, good morning." Blue glanced around the shop. Enough garments to clothe a third-world country filled every available inch of space.

"Can we help you, dear?"

"I was looking for a dress." Blue glanced down at her battered jeans and T-shirt. "Something dressy."

"Is it for a special occasion?"

"No, just dinner."

"Business or social?"

The taller woman elbowed the shorter woman in the side. "For crying out loud, Clara, just ask her if she has a hot date."

Both ladies looked at Blue and said, "Well, do you?"

Blue hid a smile behind her hand. "Yes, ma'am," she answered.

The taller woman clapped her hands together and hurried over to a jam-packed rack. "Hot damn, honey, have we got the dress for you!"

Five minutes later Blue stood in front of the dressing-room mirror, staring at her reflection in total shock. Was that her? The crimson silk dress clung to curves she'd never known she had. The front was demure from its high neckline to below-the-knee hem. The amazing part was the back. There was none. Behind her neck two silk-covered buttons held the entire dress on. There was no possible way she could wear a bra or even panty hose with it. The preacher from Cobs Corner's Baptist church would have a seizure if he saw her in it and would revoke her baptismal certificate. Her father, who had disowned her at least twice a week for nearly ten years, would sit up in his grave and call her "Jezebel." This dress was definitely designed for sins of the flesh.

Well, she wasn't in Cobs Corner any longer and her father was dead and buried. She twirled in front of the mirror. She wasn't positive, but she thought her mother would have approved.

"Lord, child," said the taller woman as she stepped out of the dressing room, "I hope your date has fire insurance."

"Why?" Blue asked.

"Because in that dress, honey, you are going to set his pants on fire."

"Martha! Blue! I found them." Clara came bustling over carrying a pair of red high-heeled sandals. "Please tell me you're a size six and a half."

Half an hour later Blue stepped out onto the sidewalk carrying a shopping bag containing the dress and shoes. While they'd plied her with tea and homemade sugar cookies, Martha and Clara had managed to pull her entire life story out of her. They were both amazed and delighted when she'd told them she was enrolled at the local college and was working part-time at Jack's Diner and as Matt's housekeeper. Clara had written down a quick and easy recipe for chicken that was guaranteed to make a grown man drool. Martha, not to be outdone, had insisted on giving her a ten-percent discount on the dress and shoes.

Blue strapped the bag onto the back of her motorcycle and put on her helmet. She was deeply grateful for the savings and the dress, and for the recipe stashed in her back pocket. Tonight she had more important things to worry about than cooking chicken for Matt. She was planning on cooking something with Matt, and chicken wasn't on the menu.

FOUR

Matt was standing in front of his bedroom mirror trying to knot his tie when he heard Blue's shower start. Visions of her standing under a downpour of water wearing nothing but soapy lather caused his hands to tremble so badly, he had to let the tie go until later.

Within half an hour he was decked out in his finest and downstairs waiting. He passed the bottom of the stairs for the fourth time and silently cursed his crutches. After an impatient glance at his watch, he glared up at the ceiling. Where was she? Granted, it was a good twenty minutes before the time he'd told her to be ready, but a little eagerness on her part would have been appreciated.

Ten minutes later Matt's heart slammed against his chest as Blue appeared at the top of the stairs. He stared transfixed as she slowly descended. She was gorgeous, and he was a dead man. Snappy red shoes adorned her feet. Trim ankles turned into shapely calves. A flair of crimson covered the rest of her legs and lovingly caressed slightly rounded hips. A narrow waist turned into luscious breasts discreetly covered by a sleeveless dress that shimmered bloodred one moment and beseeched to be caressed the next. Matt willed his heart rate to decrease to a brisk gallop and his grip on the crutches to relax. As Blue reached the bottom step he felt his Adam's apple bob up and down past the tie that was suddenly choking him.

He had to clear his throat twice before dislodging the lump of desire trapped there. "Blue, you look lovely tonight." He was in trouble. Deep, deep trouble. This date was supposed to impress upon him how unsuited they were for each other, not have him drooling down the front of his best suit.

"Thank you, Matt. You look quite debonair yourself."

She descended the last step and smiled up at him. Her blue eyes sparkled with anticipation, awareness, and desire, and he felt his resistance take a nosedive. Where was his self-control? Hell, where was his backbone? Why was it every time Blue was within five feet of him, he felt like a jellyfish sprawled at her feet? "Are you ready?" he asked with a determined smile.

"Sure. I'll go get the Bronco."

He discovered a new meaning for the phrase *backfield in motion* as he watched her walk toward the front door. *Where in the hell was the back to her dress?*

The front view was sweet, enchanting, and innocent, the perfect choice for their date. The back was
seductive, sexy, and daring. He swallowed hard. No
one, including himself, was going to believe she was
just his housekeeper. He had second and third
thoughts about going out for dinner as he watched
the sway of her enticing bottom.

"I'll meet you out front," she said, and walked
out the front door.

Matt shook his head. So much for second and
third thoughts. It looked like they were headed for
dinner, and hopefully not disaster. Sighing, he
leaned on his crutches and headed after her.

Twenty minutes later Matt allowed Blue to pre-
cede him into the cool interior of the restaurant. If
anyone was going to appreciate the view of her
back, it was going to be him. He smiled as she came
to a sudden stop and stared around the dining room
in amazement. The Green Mountain Inn had
stopped taking overnight guests just after the turn
of the century, but its kitchen had remained open
for business. The old fieldstone-and-log restaurant
was crammed with history and treasures of the past.
Deacon benches, Windsor chairs, and handmade
quilts lined the walls, along with paintings and pot-
tery. Matt saw Blue's rapt expression and chuckled.
"Do you like?"

"Oh, Matt, it's magnificent. How did you ever
find this place?" She gently touched a rag doll sitting in an antique hand-carved high chair.

"I've been coming here since I moved to Vermont, years ago. It's my favorite restaurant."

"Is the food as good as the surroundings?" Her attention turned to a miniature china tea set displayed on a small wooden table, complete with linen tablecloth. A huge cuddly teddy bear and a worn floppy-eared rabbit were waiting to be served.

"Better," he said. What was it about the children's toys that fascinated her so? he wondered. She had skipped over the artwork and finely crafted furniture, heading straight for the children's section of the huge foyer.

"Matthew!" A woman dressed in gray muslin and a brilliant white apron appeared in the doorway of the dining room. She stared at his crutches. "What happened to you?"

"Well, hello to you, too, Cora." Matt hobbled forward and planted a kiss on her wrinkled brow. "Where's Sam?"

"In the kitchen, and you didn't answer my question."

"Wrong place, wrong time," he said as Blue joined them. "That's all. Cora, I would like you to meet Blue Crawford.

"Blue, this is Cora Allan. She and her husband, Sam, own this place."

"Nice to meet you, Mrs. Allan. You have a lovely place."

"Call me Cora, please. Any friend of Matthew's is welcome here anytime." With a tsk-tsk toward the crutches she said, "Come along, you two. I don't think Matthew should be standing longer than necessary."

Matt saw a guilt-stricken look cross Blue's face and whispered, "I'm fine, Blue, don't worry."

"Are you sure?"

"Positive. The first time I brought my mother here during one of her visits, Cora and she became fast friends. Now Cora feels duty bound to fuss over me in my mother's absence."

"That's sweet."

"It's embarrassing."

Blue laughed softly and shook her head. "It would be embarrassing if she pinched your cheek and remarked on what a big boy you are. Showing concern for your leg is thoughtful and caring." She turned and followed Cora.

Matt followed the women through the main dining room, the hall that skirted the original taproom, which had been converted into another dining area, and into the small, secluded dining area that overlooked the rear gardens, vast green lawn, and the majestic Green Mountains. Cora might have been thoughtful and caring, but she was placing way too much emphasis on his dinner with Blue. This section of the restaurant was usually reserved for couples. He gave Cora a curious look as she escorted them to a corner table.

Cora grinned back. "I hope this table will do?"

Blue's gaze was locked on the view of the distant mountains. "It's wonderful, Cora."

Cora beamed as Matt held out the chair for

Blue. "I'll leave you two to enjoy your meal. Henry will be along in a minute to take your drinks order."

Matt watched as Cora hurried away. Maybe he should have explained that Blue was his housekeeper. He glanced at Blue as she read the menu and silently sighed. Cora would never have believed him and it would be insulting to Blue. He'd never had a housekeeper before, but even if he had, he doubted very much that he would have taken her out to dinner. "The house specialty is Yankee pot roast with all the trimmings," he said.

"Sounds delicious." Blue closed her menu and placed it on the table just as a young waiter approached.

While Matt glared at the handsome waiter, who seemed totally transfixed by Blue, they both ordered the house specialty. The waiter took the hint and didn't linger. "So," Matt said, toying with the stem of his water glass, "how is school going?"

"Okay, I guess. It's always a little strange starting out in a new school, trying to figure out where everything is and trying not to gawk at the other students."

"Gawk?"

"Half of them look so young, as if they shouldn't be there. Eighteen and nineteen seem like a lifetime ago." She shook her head and chuckled. "And you should see how some of them dress. Talk about rebelling against society."

He laughed at her expression. He often saw the college students when in town. Purple hair, nose rings, and clothes out of the sixties. Hell, most of the people his mother lived with in the New Age community in New Mexico dressed like that. "Every generation rebels in their own way," he said. Some of them, he added silently, never stop rebelling! He took a sip of water. "Why did you wait so long to go to college?" If she had to take on housesitting jobs and wait on tables to put herself through school, why hadn't she done it when she was nineteen?

The sparkle in her eyes dimmed. "I did a complete year at a local junior college back in Iowa, the year after I graduated from high school."

"What happened?"

"My father became ill and he needed me at home." Her gaze dropped to the table and she fingered her fork.

"I'm sorry."

She shrugged. "Life happens."

Matt felt his teeth clench. He hated that saying with a passion. He forced himself to relax. "What happened then?"

"The next year I only signed up for a few classes. The year after that a couple less, and by the third year I was only taking one class which I had to drop out of by Thanksgiving."

"There wasn't anyone who could have helped you?"

"I was his only family." She contemplated the ice cubes floating in her glass for a moment before adding, "To be perfectly honest with you, Matt, my father wasn't a very pleasant person to begin with. His illness and the ensuing helplessness only made him more disagreeable."

"All the more reason to have help. How many years did you take care of him?"

"My last year in high school I noticed a difference in him, but he refused to go to a doctor. Finally the pain got so severe he had no choice but to go. For nearly ten years he needed assistance."

"Ten years?" It sounded like a lifetime prison sentence to him. To be at a "disagreeable" man's beck and call twenty-four hours a day must have been hell. Blue hadn't mentioned one word about love. No tears filled her eyes. Just by the way she said *disagreeable*, he knew there was a lot she hadn't said.

"The first couple of years weren't so bad," she said. "I survived."

But at what cost? he wondered. "There's more to life than just surviving."

"The women's group at his church and the ladies from the local auxiliary took pity on us and were constantly bringing by casseroles, soups, desserts, and breads. You name it and they brought it."

He wondered if the womenfolk of Cobs Corner had tasted Blue's cooking and classed the contributions as a humane gesture. "That was nice and neighborly." He thought it would have been a lot more neighborly if the women had offered to take turns sitting with her father for a couple of hours every day so Blue could have some time to herself.

But then, if his own daughter thought he was miserable, Lord only knew what the townfolk thought of him. "What did he die from?"

"Emphysema." She glanced out the window at the approaching night. "You mentioned your mother. Is that her in the picture on the nightstand in the guest bedroom?"

"Yes." Blue obviously didn't want to talk about her father anymore. Shrugging, he gave her a brief description of his mother. "Veronica Stone, mother, current crystal seller, and seeker of elusive answers."

Blue smiled. "She sounds fascinating."

Matt frowned and drank more water. It figured Blue would find his mother fascinating. Birds of a feather and all that. Blue probably would patronize his mother's shop if it was within traveling distance. "Most people find my mother quite . . . uh, interesting."

"Where does she live?"

"Near Santa Fe." He saw that she really seemed interested in hearing more about his mother, so he went on. "It's a small community called Tranquility. It's referred to as a New Age development."

"Really?"

"Really. They built every building in the town out of adobe and blessings. There's communal bathing in the river. All the children are home-schooled and they practice healing with herbs."

"So when you said your mother sells crystal, you

weren't referring to wineglasses and brandy snifters."

Matt laughed. "No. My mother owns a crystal and fragrance shop. She sells hunks of rocks to overstressed executives looking for inner peace and the meaning of life?"

"Is that the question she's seeking an answer to? The meaning of life."

"No. My mother is still trying to understand why my father died."

Blue was quiet for a long moment. "Why did your father die?" she asked softly.

He knew the answer to that, even if his mother didn't. "Because he was a flyboy for the U.S. Air Force during the Vietnam War. Uncle Sam said go, so he went." Matt picked up his water glass and watched as the ice clinked against the side. The memory of the last time he saw his father was faded and blurred. He no longer trusted what was fact and what was a child's imagination.

"My mother and I said good-bye to him at Travis Air Force Base, outside of San Francisco. I can still remember—it was the only time I ever saw my mother cry. She didn't cry even when he was sent home in a flag-draped coffin and given a military funeral. She just stood there dry-eyed, saying one word over and over again. Why?" He glanced away from the glass and managed a halfhearted smile. "Captain Michael Stone died because it was his job. He always knew it was part of the job. To give his life for his country."

"How old were you then?"

"Five. I had just started kindergarten when he was called overseas. We received a visit from a chaplain on New Year's Day."

"I'm sorry, Matt."

He shrugged. He didn't know how to respond to her sympathy. Faded photographs and a distant memory were all he had left of his father. He couldn't even say he missed him. How could you miss a person you couldn't remember?

The waiter placed their salads in front of them and faded away. Matt wasn't comfortable talking about his family, so he threw the ball back into her court. Any relationship concerning a father intrigued him. He had always wondered how his life might have turned out if Michael Stone had lived. "Did you and your father have a close relationship?"

"Lord no." Blue chuckled. "I was a total disappointment to my father."

"A disappointment? I find that hard to believe." Any young woman who cared for an ailing father for ten years could never be classed a disappointment in his book. "What did you do that was so wrong?"

"I wasn't your typical Cobs Corner daughter." Blue munched on a piece of lettuce and smiled.

"What's a typical Cobs Corner daughter?"

"Let's see. . . ." She waved her fork. "First she graduates from high school. Then she works for about a year down at the local Piggly Wiggly as a cashier. Then she marries her high-school sweetheart and produces a grandchild every eighteen months or so for the next ten years."

Matt laughed at her expression. She looked like she would rather walk through a roomful of rattlesnakes than be a typical Cobs Corner daughter. "What disappointed him the most, that you didn't become a cashier, or that you didn't marry your high-school sweetheart?"

"My single status was a thorn in his side. I was an embarrassment to him because I refused to follow the same path every other female in Cobs Corner took. According to my father, a woman's place was in her home, under the rule of her husband, surrounded by dirty laundry, cookie dough, and half a dozen babies."

Matt couldn't contain the slight irritation in his voice when he asked, "Did your father have anyone in particular in mind?"

"Oh, yes. His name was Caleb Willing and he owned the farm next to ours."

Matt felt the cherry tomato he'd just eaten drop down his throat, squeeze past his tie, and make a ten-point landing in the pit of his stomach. He sipped some water before trying to talk. "What did this Caleb think of your father's idea?"

"At first he gave it some serious thought."

"You were going to marry a man your father picked out?"

"I wasn't going to marry Caleb."

"Why not?"

Blue sighed and shook her head. "For the same reason Caleb wasn't going to marry me. No spark."

Matt studied the beautiful and seemingly intelligent woman calmly eating her salad and wondered if he should ask the next question. Curiosity was killing him, though. He had to know. "What does 'no spark' mean?"

"Do you have a sister?"

"No, I'm an only child."

"Okay, pretend you had a sister." She munched on a sliced cucumber. "Now imagine you're kissing her."

"She's my sister!"

"Now you know what no spark is."

Matt's gaze focused on her tongue as she licked her lower lip, leaving behind a shiny combination of moisture, oil, vinegar, and lipstick. His voice husky, he said, "Tell me what spark is."

She pushed away her empty plate and stared out into the night. "Spark is the beginning. It's the start of something. Everything begins with a spark. A relationship must have that spark to grow and develop into something wonderful."

"And you didn't have this spark with Caleb?"

"No. What we have is a deep friendship and an understanding. We've been there for each other all our lives, and in our own way we love each other, but it's the wrong kind of love to build a marriage on."

He wondered just how deep an "understanding" Caleb and Blue had shared. For some unexplainable reason, he was resentful of Caleb, sparks or no sparks. It shouldn't matter to him what Blue had done in the past, but it did. He frowned at his wayward thoughts as the waiter removed the salad plates and set their dinners in front of them.

Blue dug into the pot roast and smiled. "This is heavenly. I wonder if Cora would give me the recipe."

Matt thought about all the cows that lined up for the honor of being part of Cora's Yankee pot roast and shuddered. There definitely would be a stampede in the opposite direction if they found out Blue was going to be the cook. "I'm not sure. I think the recipe has been in her family for generations. You know how temperamental cooks can be."

Blue shrugged and pushed some food around on her plate. "I've been thinking."

"About what?"

"I really should be doing more for you."

Matt forced himself to swallow. "What do you want to do for me?" His body could think of a dozen possible responses to that question. He prayed his expression didn't betray his body.

"I should be cooking and cleaning more. So far you've cooked a roast and taken me to dinner. I, on the other hand, managed to pick up pizza last night."

Sounded like a good deal to him. After eating her eggs and pancakes, he wasn't sure if his stomach was up to handling a complete dinner from her. "Let's not talk about our deal tonight."

"But I haven't had the chance to do anything around the house."

"Blue, please. Let's enjoy the night." She looked like she was about to argue some more, so he quickly added, "I have no regrets about our arrangement, do you?"

"No, it's just—"

"Are you always this argumentative?"

"I'm not argumentative." She stabbed a potato with her fork. "There is something I've been meaning to ask you."

"What's that?"

"Since you're the computer expert, would you teach me to 'surf the net'?"

He grinned. "I'll have you surfing like a pro come Halloween."

She grinned back. "I have to warn you, I'm about as adept with a keyboard as I am with a frying pan."

He must not have controlled his expression because Blue's laughter filled their corner of the dining room.

An hour later Blue was completely lost. "Are you sure you know where we are?" They had left the restaurant fifteen minutes earlier, and Matt had been directing her deeper into the mountains.

"Slow down, you might miss the turnoff."

"Honestly, Matt, we are on top of a mountain. Where do you expect to turn?" As far as she could tell, any turn would have them plunging off the dark mountaintop.

"There it is." He pointed out the windshield toward the right. "Just past that group of trees."

"*What* group of trees? The whole mountain is nothing *but* trees."

"There." His finger jabbed the glass. "See it?"

"Now I do." She turned onto a small black-topped area and sucked in her breath as she stopped the vehicle. They were on top of the world! Miles and miles of pine-covered mountains, deep valleys, and brilliant stars surrounded them. "It's beautiful!" She had seen some wondrous sights since she'd left Iowa, but none as breathtaking as this. "How did you find this place?"

"It's on all the tourist maps, but very few people come up here at night." He gave the spectacular view a fleeting glance before returning his gaze to her. "I come up here sometimes just to get my perspective on the world back."

She glanced away from the view. "Is your perspective out again?"

"Not tonight. There's another reason why I wanted to come here tonight."

She noticed how serious he was and wondered if she was about to be fired. "What's that?"

"I want to kiss you."

She laughed with relief. "You made me drive you all the way up here just so you could kiss me?"

"I didn't want to kiss you at home."

"Why not?"

"Because I don't want you to think me kissing you has anything to do with our arrangement. If you don't want me to kiss you, just say so, and we'll pretend this never happened."

Blue bit her lip to keep from smiling. Matt appeared so serious and polite. Here he had been afraid to make a pass at her back at the house for fear she would consider it sexual harassment. Wasn't that the sweetest thing? He'd been attracted to her all along.

She unsnapped her seat belt. "What do we do if I want to kiss you back?"

His seat belt came unsnapped. He reached out and wound a golden curl around his finger. "Did I tell you how beautiful you look tonight?"

She leaned in closer and smiled. "Twice, but who's counting?"

His laugh feathered her lips an instant before he claimed them for his own.

FIVE

The moon climbed higher and the stars seemed to twinkle brighter over the Green Mountains as the couple embraced.

Blue leaned into Matt's demanding hold and welcomed its warmth. As his tongue traced her lower lip she sank her fingers into his chestnut hair and deepened the kiss. His tongue swept into her mouth as a ragged groan emerged from his throat.

She felt his hand travel the length of her bare back before sliding around to rest upon her hip. Fire seemed to flare in its wake. Her whole body came alive with his slightest touch. She wanted more. Her hand slowly lowered onto his chest. She could feel the rapid pounding of his heart through the cottony softness of his shirt.

He tore his mouth away from hers and drew a ragged breath. "Sparks?" he asked.

She leaned back from him to study his face. In

the dim interior of the Bronco it was difficult to see him, but she didn't really need to. His face was engraved into her memory. It haunted her dreams. She could feel the slight trembling of his hands and hear his harsh breathing echoing in the confines of the truck. Matt was just as affected by the kiss as she was. Smiling what she hoped was a seductive smile, she pulled his head back to hers and whispered, "Inferno."

The second kiss proved to her how tame and civil the first kiss had been. Hot, raw passion exploded between them. It was like nothing she had ever experienced before. She felt herself dissolve in a vortex of desire. There was only Matt, only this feeling of unexplainable need.

She finally understood. This was the turbulent sensation poets had been writing about since the beginning of time. She pulled Matt closer as they sank down onto the seat.

Her gasp of pleasure filled the air as he gently cupped one breast.

He raised his head and gazed down at her. She could see the burning hunger blazing in his gaze and knew it matched her own. A streak of fire raced through her body as his thumb skimmed her rigid nipple. She blessed the fact that she hadn't worn a bra.

With great care he slid his hand behind her neck and undid the two buttons there. Then he paused, apparently waiting for her to protest. He would wait forever. She couldn't protest; she could barely breathe.

As he slowly lowered the front of her dress she felt the cool night air caress her heated skin and wondered at the contrast. Wasn't this when she was supposed to put a stop to what they were doing? Why was it feeling so right with Matt? Other men had kissed her, but she had never felt this yearning to know more. To experience more. Never had she felt this need to know the secrets of making love.

She watched, fascinated, as Matt lowered his head and took her nipple into his mouth. Heat erupted as his tongue flicked at the sensitive nub. A curious feeling of emptiness started at the base of her stomach and moved lower to the core of her womanhood. The sensation pulsated to the rhythm he had set with every pull of his mouth against her breast.

In a rustle of silk they lay down on the seat. He released her nipple and claimed her mouth. Blue gloried in the pressure of his weight resting lightly across her body. His arousal was pressed against her thigh, mere inches from her emptiness. Excitement sparked and flared through her veins as his large hand slid up her bare leg. Her thighs parted willingly as she opened her mouth to deepen the kiss.

Somewhere in the back of her mind it registered that they were in the front seat of his Bronco and that anyone could come along and see them. She didn't care. Matt's fingers caressed the insides of her thighs, streaking higher with every stroke. He released her mouth, and she greedily sucked in much-needed oxygen as his lips caressed her chin, her throat, and the valley between her breasts. When his fingers encountered her silk panties, he angled his kisses toward her pouting nipples.

She pushed her hips against his hand and silently cursed the silken barrier as the ache inside her intensified. Moisture coated her panties as Matt eased a finger inside the lace edges. She opened her legs wider and felt the heat of his finger. A moan of pure pleasure escaped her lips as he slipped his finger into the emptiness inside her.

At the sound of her moan, he raised his head. "Blue?" His voice sounded hoarse with desire, but there was a hint of uncertainty too. He started to remove his hand.

She squeezed her thighs together and lifted her hips higher, until he was once again inside. "No, don't stop." When she saw Matt was trying to regain control, she shamelessly begged, "Please." Nothing like this had ever happened to her before. She needed to know where this would end.

He kissed the tip of her nose. "I won't stop. I promise."

She closed her eyes and let the waves of pleasure wash over her as his hand quickened its rhythm and she soared higher. His hot breath mingled with hers as she raced toward an ending she didn't understand but knew she had to reach. The higher she soared, the more frightened she became. What if she never reached it? "Matt!"

A second finger joined the first and the pace intensified. "It's okay, Blue. I have you."

She reached the crest and teetered on the edge. "But . . ." Something wasn't right. She wanted Matt with her. She wanted him to soar with her.

He pressed his free hand against her shaking head. "Let it come, Blue. Let it come."

Her cry of release was seized and savored by his mouth.

A long time later Blue blinked several times to clear the remaining fog. They were still tangled and twisted like pretzels in the front seat of the Bronco. The windows were thick with steam. The breathtaking view was lost behind the coating of condensation and she felt like a guilty teenager. Lord knew why. She had never done anything like this when she *was* a teenager.

She glanced down at her semidressed self and quickly closed her eyes. She could feel the flush of embarrassment sweep up her entire body as she fumbled with her dress and hastily rebuttoned the buttons. One quick look at Matt only made the flush deepen. The man had just given her the most incredible experience in her life and he was completely dressed. He still had his suit jacket on, and not one button on his shirt was undone. The only sign of what had just transpired was his mussed hair and slightly crooked tie. She wanted the leather seat to open up and swallow her whole.

"Blue?" He maneuvered himself away from her as she sat up, brushing her dress back down over her thighs.

She avoided looking at him and studied the steering wheel directly in front of her. *What in the hell had just happened?* Scratch that, she knew what had happened. Matt knew what had happened. All the wildlife within a hundred yards knew what had happened. She closed her eyes and gave thanks that at least the windows had been rolled up. If they hadn't been, her cry of pleasure would still be echoing off the mountaintops. She wasn't just embarrassed, she was mortified beyond belief.

"Blue?"

The tender concern in Matt's voice tore at her control. What was she supposed to do now? Thank him? Cook him breakfast? Smoke a cigarette? Lord, she didn't know if she could face him, let alone hold a conversation. She glanced at the crooked knot in his tie. "Yes?"

Matt felt his heart give a funny little lurch. Blue couldn't even meet his eyes. He ignored the pain burning in his right thigh and slid closer. "I gather this is all pretty new for you," he said, brushing a curl away from her flushed cheek. Could Blue be a novice to the pleasures of love?

She kept her gaze lowered, worried her lower lip, and shrugged.

He cupped her chin and raised her face to his. "There's nothing to be embarrassed about, Blue." He brushed her kiss-swollen mouth with his own.

"What happened was completely natural between a man and a woman." He didn't consider it too natural to happen on the first date, not considering their ages and where they were. But he didn't think Blue would appreciate his opinion on the subject right now. Anyway, he was trying to get her to at least look at him. Something magical had happened when he'd kissed her. Something he wanted to experience again when he was in a more appropriate location. Blue was right. There had been not only sparks, but a complete inferno between them.

He gently pulled her into his embrace and wondered where they were going to go from here. He smiled into the darkness as she sighed and relaxed in his arms.

A few minutes of silence went by before she finally spoke. It wasn't anything profound, just a simple request. "Do you think we could crack a window? It's awfully hot in here."

"Start the engine and turn the air conditioner on. The mosquitoes will eat us alive if I open the window."

He watched as she started the Bronco, then she slipped back into his embrace. When the windshield cleared she hesitantly asked, "Wasn't I supposed to do something?"

Full-blown laughter erupted from him. When he was able to control himself, he asked, "About what?"

She gestured wildly with one hand. "You know about what!" He started laughing again, and she howled, "For cripesake, Matt, you still have your tie on!"

He really did try to control his laughter, but it was like holding back time. When he felt Blue stiffen in his arms he cupped her flushed cheeks in his hands. "Something special happened tonight, Blue." He ran one thumb over her trembling lower lip. Lord, he wanted to kiss her until next week, next month, next year.

"For me maybe," she said, "but what about you?"

Matt frowned. What did she mean by *maybe?* She had to have felt the magic! Nothing that explosive could be all one-sided. He was still hard and throbbing, but what they had just experienced was special, extraordinary. He'd never had a woman shatter so completely at his touch. "The next time, Blue, I'll be with you." He sealed his vow with a gentle brush of his mouth across hers.

"Is there going to be a next time?"

He would have given half his computer equipment to see her face more clearly. He couldn't tell if the prospect of there being a next time excited her, or made her uneasy. Her voice had been curiously reserved. "Only you know the answer to that one, Blue."

"Me?"

"Yes, you." He released her face and tried to maneuver his leg into a more comfortable position. "I'm all for there being a next time, and a time after that, and a time after that. Hell, the way I feel right now, once you're in my bed, don't plan on leaving it until you're seventy, possibly eighty years old." He brushed a curl away from the corner of her mouth. "But the decision to come to my bed will be entirely yours. I don't want you to feel pressured, just because you're living in my house."

"You don't think our living together will affect my decision?"

He couldn't be sure, but he thought he heard amusement in her voice. "Well," he said, "let's put it this way. I'm hoping that by seeing me every day and night, you won't stand a chance against my charms."

"Charms?"

Now he was positive there was laughter in her voice. The little witch. Here he was aching for her, and all he wanted to do was to hear her laugh again. What kind of spell had she cast over him? "Yeah, charms. I've been known to possess one or two."

She pressed her cheek against his chest and snuggled closer. "Just one or two?"

"On my good days." He was tempted to kiss her again, just to show her a charm or two. He needed to get them off this mountain and back into some sort of civilization before he embarrassed himself by begging. "Are you ready for dessert yet?" She had refused dessert back at the restaurant. Maybe now she had recharged her appetite.

He could feel her smile against his shirt. "What do you have in mind?"

The blood rushing through his veins heated past

the boiling point as her fingers toyed with a button on his shirt. "Ice cream," he said, his voice unnaturally strained.

Blue sank farther into the front seat and ran her tongue around the edge of her cone. "This is the best ice cream I have ever tasted."

Matt watched her lick the side of the cone and silently groaned. How could such an innocent gesture cause such a riot to his hormones? Stopping at the local ice-cream stand outside of Greenhaven had seemed like a good idea fifteen minutes ago. Now, after seeing how Blue ate an ice-cream cone, he wasn't too sure. "It's all homemade," he said, then nodded toward the late-night crowd of boisterous teenagers at Dairy Heaven. "Thanks for standing in line."

"Why didn't you tell me your leg was bothering you? We could have headed straight back home."

"It will be fine once I unfold it from this sardine can." He didn't want to talk about his leg. He didn't like this feeling of helplessness. He especially didn't like it around Blue, which was strange considering that if it hadn't been for the accident and the ensuing helplessness, he never would have met her.

"Are you sure you're going to be all right? Maybe we should find a doctor."

"It's just cramped up, Blue. Relax." He gave her a reassuring smile. "A couple of laps in the pool when we get home will work wonders." Silently he added, *on more than just my leg*.

They ate without speaking for a few minutes. Blue was reaching for her seat belt after quickly finishing her cone when he stopped her. "You have ice cream on your chin." He caught her hand as she was reaching for a napkin. He couldn't resist the temptation and pulled her across the seat toward him. "I'll get it."

He cupped the back of her neck and brought her closer, then used his tongue to remove the drop of chocolate that smeared her chin. Smiling, he pulled back and examined his handiwork. "All gone."

"Thank you."

With the luminous parking lights he could see the desire in the depths of her eyes. "My pleasure." He placed a small kiss on the tip of her nose, released her, and leaned back into his seat. "Home, James."

She shook her head. "I think you're beginning to like being waited on."

His wide grin was his only response.

Twenty minutes later Blue pulled as close to the front door as she could and demanded, "You wait there. I'll be right around."

Before she could make it around the front of the Bronco, Matt had retrieved his crutches from the backseat and was trying to heave himself into a standing position. "I told you to wait," she scolded as she joined him by the passenger door.

Clearly frustrated and in pain, he snapped, "I can do it myself." She stood helplessly by and watched as he tried to straighten his leg. With the help of his crutches he finally stood. He took a steadying breath and smiled. "See, I told you I could do it."

She ignored the little-boy smile that could melt any woman's heart. "Macho bullcrap," she snapped. "There's nothing wrong with accepting a little help when you need it, dunderhead." She could think of at least a dozen other names to call him, any of which, according to her late father, would see her straight to hell for eternity. "Now, do you think you can make it to the house and into your swimming trunks, then into the pool, without my help?"

His smile was pure mischief. "I might need some help getting into my swimming suit. It's a tricky little devil."

She slammed the passenger door shut and stormed around the front of the Bronco. "And to think I was concerned, silly me." She got back into the truck and without looking back headed it for the garage.

Five minutes later she entered the house just as Matt emerged from the downstairs powder room wearing his bathing suit and carrying a towel. His face still looked pinched with pain, and guilt assaulted her once again. Here she had been contemplating jumping the poor man's bones, and he could barely walk! Her smile hesitant, she asked, "Do you need any help getting to the pool?"

"No, I'm fine. It's already starting to feel better just by walking on it. I'm sure it will be good as new after a couple of laps." He grimaced as some of his weight landed on the sore leg. "Well, as good as could be expected." He opened the sliding doors to the back deck. "Thanks for being concerned, though. It's nice to know there's someone here in case I really do need help."

"Anytime. Just give a holler." She didn't want to ruin the moment by reminding him that she was getting free room and board in exchange for her assistance. Something magical had happened that night that had nothing to do with free room and board or her domestic abilities.

She watched as he made his way down the steps to the deck below. He seemed to be getting around better. He tossed his white towel onto a recliner and laid both crutches onto the deck. She gazed pensively at the shimmering water as he dived into the pool. Had it really been only a few days since they'd met in that pool? It seemed longer.

When he started swimming without any notice-able strain, she turned away from the patio doors and made her way upstairs.

Cool water helped to dampen Matt's arousal and the exercise eased the tension in his thigh. He reached the shallow end of the pool and used his good leg to push off the wall. He planned on swimming himself beyond exhaustion.

Upon completing his eighth lap, he clung to the edge of the pool and caught his breath. Blue filled his every sense. If he closed his eyes tightly enough, he could almost taste her and hear those sweet purrs that vibrated from her throat when she was excited. He could practically smell the lotion she had applied to her smooth skin and the flowery fragrance of her shampoo. His hand reached out to caress her, met only air, and he slipped under the water. He muttered an obscenity as he surfaced.

Blue was driving him crazy! He heaved his tired body from the water and wearily reached for his crutches. As he returned to the house he cursed his leg. He didn't like being confined to crutches and couldn't wait for the day he could burn the pair he now needed. A frown wrinkled his brow as he entered the kitchen. If he no longer needed the crutches, he would no longer need Blue to stay. It was one hell of a dilemma.

He opened the back door to retrieve the cats' empty food dish and was greeted by Raven. "Hello, girl. Miss me?" He took the meow and the rubbing up against his bare calf as a positive response. "I hear you gals have been leaving some interesting presents for Blue."

"Meow."

"The field mice are bad enough. Just don't bring any more snakes. I don't think Blue likes them, even if they are dead."

"Meow."

He reached down and scratched Raven behind the ear. "Where's Moondancer?"

Raven seemed to give him a look of exasperation, as if to say, *You know how she is.*

Chuckling, he scratched behind the other black ear. "I know, she does get a little strange at night. That's why I named her Moondancer. Why don't you try coming around during the day so Blue can meet you?"

"Meow."

"Sure, sure. You tell me that all the time. Come on in while I get your food."

He left the back door open and went to fill the dish. Raven came slowly into the kitchen. Never taking her eyes off the back door, she sniffed around under the table. In all the years he had lived there, Raven had never gone farther into the house than the kitchen. Moondancer had never once entered the house.

Raven, who was entirely black, had shown up one day during the construction of his home. Every night she would devour a bowl of cat food and then be on her way.

Moondancer was a different story. She'd been no more than a kitten when he'd found her under his Bronco one winter day trying to keep warm. With the fierceness of a lion, she'd refused to be held or comforted. He'd left a bowl of food and water where she could find it. The next morning the bowls had been empty except for the dead mouse in one of them.

Unsure if Raven or the kitten had left the "thank you," he had started to put out twice as much food each night. The more food he left, the bigger the "thank you." One night his curiosity had gotten the better of him. After placing the dishes on the patio, he sat in a chair by the window and waited.

Half an hour later a fluffy orange kitten came dancing out of the woods. She pranced, skipped, and did a kitten version of the Texas two-step till she reached the food. Laughing, he watched as she devoured half the food in the dish. After cleaning her paws and whiskers, she frolicked back across the patio and disappeared into the woods.

As a black shadow crossed the patio, he knew Raven was about to get her share. Neither cat had brought a "thank you," though. With a feeling of disappointment, he started to move away from the window when a movement caught his attention.

In total amazement he watched as Moondancer, that cute frolicsome kitten, dragged a dead crow across the patio. Since the crow was too big for the bowl, Moondancer dumped it by the now empty dish.

Openmouthed, he watched as Raven turned up her nose at the bird, turned her back on the merry little kitten, and marched into the woods. If Moondancer was upset by Raven's snub, she didn't show it. She bounced over the patio, rolled over twice, smiled up at the moon, and with a sway of her hips disappeared into the night's shadows.

That was when he'd named her Moondancer. She had not changed much in two years. She still left "thank you" presents, and only on rare occasions had he seen her in the light of day.

Matt finished filling the bowl with food and headed for the back door, only to discover Raven had beaten him outside. He placed the bowl on the patio and patted the cat on top of the head before going back inside. Years ago when he'd adopted Raven, he had taken her to the local vet and made sure she would never be burdened with trying to raise a family in the wild.

Moondancer was another story. To look at her, one would never suspect she lived in the wild. Her orange-striped fur was always immaculate and her sparkling green eyes always seemed to be laughing. She appeared dainty and ladylike, but he knew the true Moondancer. He had seen her drag dead rodents twice her size across a hundred-yard clearing, then dance around them.

He locked the back door and turned off the lights. Any male cat brave enough to try to mate with Moondancer was in for one mighty big surprise. Matt's cats had always seemed a little strange to Jared and his other friends. They were used to soft playful felines who curled up at your feet on cold winter's nights. No one had understood his fondness for the two wild cats, except his mother. Veronica understood his need to nurture the cats, to give them a home, as best he could and as much as they would accept. Blue understood too. She never questioned his choice of pets. Her only complaint had been Moondancer's twisted sense of payment.

He made sure all the doors were locked and the lights turned off before heading for his room. This wasn't a good sign. He didn't want Blue to understand him. It would be too personal. He muttered a curse as he hobbled his way down the hall and passed Blue's closed bedroom door. As if what had happened in the front seat of his Bronco earlier wasn't *too personal*!

Why was he worrying about Blue's reaction to his cats when he had larger problems to worry about? Such as, why was his head telling him to forget Blue, that she was all wrong for him, when his heart was telling him to take a chance on her?

SIX

A week later Matt awoke with a pounding headache and a sense of loneliness. It was after seven and Blue was scheduled to work the breakfast shift at the diner. Then she had classes until four. He'd be lucky to spend an hour with her before she had to start in on homework. The day hadn't even begun and already he missed her. He couldn't believe it had been a week since their date. If he hadn't seen firsthand how busy Blue was, he would have sworn she was trying to avoid him.

He doubted if he had spent more than five hours in her company the entire week. If it hadn't been for hastily eaten dinners and his weekly doctor appointment, it probably wouldn't have been that much time. Blue was a whirling tornado, always on the move, while he hobbled around on crutches and was confined to the house and pool. At least all the exercises were paying off. He could now maneuver himself with the help of only one crutch. By the end of the week he might need only a cane. By Halloween there was an excellent chance he wouldn't need even that.

Sighing, he pushed himself out of bed, stepped into a pair of jeans, and headed downstairs for a cup of coffee. Maybe the caffeine would clear the fog from his brain. Getting by with only a few hours of sleep every night was costing him. Something had to give, and give soon. Raging frustration was keeping him up practically every night. He wanted Blue in his bed.

He had just made it down the stairs when a knock sounded on the front door. It had to be Jared. He was the only one who periodically stopped in at this hour of the morning. Heading for the door, Matt hollered, "Hold on, I'm coming!"

He opened the front door and scowled at his grinning friend. "Cripes, Jared, how does Alison stand you in the morning?" He was beginning to hate cheerful people in the morning.

If it was possible, Jared's smile widened as he entered the house. "It's called love, my dear friend." Jared's hand immediately reached into the candy bowl for a fistful of M&M's. "You ought to try it sometime."

Matt continued to glare and allowed the screen door to slam shut. The one thing he didn't need was another lecture from Jared on all the wonders of marriage. He'd been hearing enough of them since Jared had taken the plunge two years earlier. There was only one thing worse than an ex-smoker preaching to other smokers, and that was an ex–confirmed bachelor preaching to the remaining single male population.

Matt had nothing against the institution of marriage; in fact, he would love to join it one day and start a family. But he was missing the key ingredient—a wife! The perfect woman hadn't, as yet, entered his life. He ignored the tiny voice in the back of his head taunting him that maybe she had and he was just too blind to see. Blue wasn't the perfect woman. She couldn't be the one.

"I'll get married," he muttered, more to himself than to Jared, "just as soon as Ms. Right makes her appearance." He hobbled toward the kitchen. "Are you staying for coffee?"

"Since you asked so nicely, how could I refuse?" Jared followed him into the kitchen. "Down to one crutch, I see. How's the leg?"

"Improving." Matt picked up the note Blue had left on the kitchen table. *Breakfast in the microwave. Lunch on top shelf of refrigerator. Dinner will be at six. Blue.* Short, impersonal, and to the point. The damn note could have been written by a real housekeeper. Frustration pulled at his gut. What did she think the other night had been all about?

"Matt?"

"Sorry, Jared." He cleared his mind as his friend's voice registered. "Did you say something?"

Jared shook his head and studied his friend. "Nothing important."

Matt tossed the note onto the counter and dumped the still-warm pot of coffee down the drain.

"Hey, Matt. Are you sure you're okay?"

Matt rinsed out the glass container and started a fresh pot. "Ever taste paint thinner?"

"Can't say that I have." Jared pulled down two coffee mugs. "Blue's coffee isn't that bad at the diner."

"Jack probably doesn't let her go near the machine."

Jared scanned the note Matt had thrown on the counter and headed for the microwave. "She can't be that bad of a cook." He opened the black glass door and stared inside.

Matt saw the look of horror on his friend's face and chuckled. "Please tell me it isn't French toast again. NASA could have used the last batch she made as heat-shielding tiles for the space shuttles."

"Uh, it isn't French toast."

"Oh, Lord, not pancakes again!"

"No."

"Okay, Jared, the suspense is killing me. What is it?"

"I'm not sure." He carefully lifted the bowl out of the microwave and placed it on the counter. He tried pulling the spoon from the gray blob. "Concrete?"

Matt studied the bowl of gray lumpy stuff, topped with two strawberries and a sprig of parsley, and groaned. "I think it's supposed to be oatmeal."

"How can you tell?"

"What else could it be?" He poured the coffee and handed a cup to Jared. "Remember, it's supposed to be breakfast."

"Are you going to eat it?" Jared gave a hard yank and the spoon left the gray mass with a sick sucking sound.

Matt looked at Jared as if he had lost his mind. "You try it first and tell me how it is."

Jared added cream to his coffee. "Won't Blue know?"

Matt raised one eyebrow. "Are you going to tell her I didn't eat it?"

Jared shuddered and pushed the bowl away. "No way, buddy." He glanced curiously at the refrigerator. "Should I look and see what's on the menu for lunch?"

"In all the years I have known you, I've never realized what a sadistic streak you have." Matt took his first sip of coffee and sighed with pleasure. This was more like it. While Blue's coffee improved with each pot she brewed, it still wasn't there yet. By Halloween she should have coffee down pat, and maybe by Thanksgiving she would actually be able to scramble a few eggs without either burning them or making them crunchy. There was no telling what kind of culinary skills she could develop over time.

Matt frowned and set his coffee on the counter. Time was something they didn't have. Blue was only staying until the end of the semester. By Christmas she would be gone. He wasn't even sure if she would stay in this state, let alone in this part of the country. She would be heading to wherever the next housesitting job was. Packing up everything and following the road. Just like his mother.

"Hey, Matt."

Matt shook his head to clear the vision of Blue leaving and blinked at his friend. "I'm sorry, Jared." He shrugged. "Just gathering dust." Jared looked ready to haul him down to the station and give him a drug test. Matt couldn't blame him. He definitely hadn't been himself lately.

"I asked how Blue is as a housekeeper," Jared said. "I've already witnessed her culinary skills. Is she any better at whatever it is housekeepers do?"

"She could be, if she had the time." Matt rooted through a cabinet until he found a box of cereal. Why had Blue put canned vegetables and a bear-shaped plastic bottle of honey on the cereal shelf? Half the time he couldn't find anything in his own kitchen. "She's so busy between her college courses, working at Jack's, homework, and running me all over the place, there isn't a whole lot of time for dusting, cleaning, and other housekeeping stuff."

"So why are you allowing her to stay if she isn't doing the work?"

Matt glared at his too-knowing friend. "Don't you have citizens to protect and serve?"

Jared downed his remaining coffee and chuckled. "I know when I'm not wanted." He placed the empty cup in the sink and headed for the front door. "My advice to you, buddy, is don't fight it."

Matt followed Jared into the living room. "Fight what?"

Jared grinned. "There aren't too many reasons why a man would employ a housekeeper whose every meal could be his last and who doesn't even clean."

"She needed a place to stay, Jared. So drop it." He didn't like the direction this conversation was headed.

"Taking in more strays, are you?"

He knew Jared was referring to Raven and Moondancer. "Blue's not a stray! She's a mature woman, a college student, a waitress, and currently my housekeeper."

Jared grabbed another handful of candy before opening the door. "Did you ever notice her legs? For being such a tiny thing she has incredibly long legs." Jared popped a red M&M into his mouth and grinned again. "I guess you haven't noticed them, her being your housekeeper and all."

Matt continued to scowl at the screen door long after he'd heard Jared's police cruiser pull out of the driveway. He didn't know what upset him more; that Jared had seen right through him and his interest in Blue, or that his best friend had been checking out her legs. For two cents he would pick up the phone and have a nice little chat with Alison. That would put a quick end to Jared's wandering eyes.

That evening Blue finally relaxed as Matt pushed away his empty plate and groaned with satisfaction. Dinner had been a success and Matt hadn't seemed to mind that she had stopped at a Chinese restaurant for takeout. After her last class had ended at four, she'd had to dash to the library to pick up a book. She hadn't counted on meeting up with a group of students from her psych class and getting pulled into a discussion about television and the effects it was having on children. By the time she'd realized the time, it had been too late to cook something and have it ready by six. One of the students had recommended the Chinese restaurant near campus. She had hurried over to the Kung Fung Palace and ordered up dinner for two to go.

She glanced at the empty white containers and grinned. "Here I thought you might not like Chinese." Matt had devoured everything. There wasn't a speck of sweet and sour pork or a chow mein noodle left to be seen.

He grinned in return. "I told you I like just about everything."

"You didn't mind an assortment of cartons for dinner?" Guilt was a heavy burden to carry, and she was bearing an enormous load. Here she was Matt's housekeeper, and she couldn't even cook the guy a decent meal. The poor man was stuck in the house all day long, doing Lord only knew what in his office, and she fed him soggy egg rolls and cryptic fortune cookies.

Another part of her guilt came from knowing

she was trying to avoid Matt as much as possible. It was difficult, considering they were living in the same house. She had requested more hours from Jack, telling herself it was for the purchase of a car when deep down inside she knew that was only a partial truth. More accurately, she simply had no idea how to act, or what to say to Matt after what had happened the other night.

She was still embarrassed by her behavior, her uninhibited response to Matt's touch. Nothing like that had ever happened to her before. The confusing part was, she wanted it to happen again, but with a different ending. The next time she wanted Matt to be with her for every glorious minute. But he no longer seemed interested. Not by one word or deed had he shown that he even remembered what had happened in the front seat of his Bronco. It was both humiliating and insulting. And it was driving her crazy. Had she done something wrong?

"Are you going to need me around tomorrow night?" she asked as she started to clear the table, throwing away the empty cartons.

"Why?"

"I need to spend some time in the computer lab at school." She dropped the forks into the plastic compartment inside the dishwasher. "It's the last place I would like to be, but some things can't be helped."

"Why's it the last place you'd like to be?"

"I know it's your job to work with them, but I

can't help it." She rinsed the plates and placed them in the machine.

"Help what?"

"I feel intimidated by them, by computers." Matt pushed back from the table as she wiped it down. "They just seem so damn smart."

He chuckled. "Sorry to disillusion you, Blue, but a computer is as dumb as a rock."

"I've seen the 'rocks' cluttering your office, Matt. There isn't a dumb one among them."

"There're only three, and of course there isn't a dumb one among them. I wrote most of the programs for them myself."

She didn't like the look entering Matt's eyes. He seemed to be reading her mind. She turned away and busied herself with cleaning the counters. She didn't want him to see how terrified she really was of computers. Her high school hadn't had any. The basic computer course she had taken her first year of college nearly ten years ago was so outdated, it was virtually useless. For every year she had stayed away from school, she'd fallen further and further behind. Most of the time she felt as if she would never catch up. The students she went to school with now owned their own computers. Half of them even carried their "laptops" or "notebooks" to class with them. How could she admit to them she was floundering in a sea of technology? Matt's sea.

"You don't have to drive all the way to school if you don't want to," he said.

"I don't?"

"You can use one of mine. They're all connected to the Internet, so you can access anything you might need."

"Thanks for the offer, but I wouldn't want to mess anything up." She preferred the computer lab on campus because there was always somebody there who could answer her questions. She tended to have a lot of questions.

"You won't mess anything up." He stood up and reached for his one crutch. "Come on, I'll show you which one you can use." He started for the doorway.

"Wait!" She worried her lower lip for a second. "There's something you should know."

"What's that?"

"I'm not very good with computers." There, she'd said it. She had finally admitted to him that she was a klutz with the equipment he made his living from. Matt spent hours every day immersed in a world she didn't understand. A world made up of bits and bytes.

"All you need is practice," he said.

"I don't know about that." Her cooking skills hadn't improved in all the years she'd taken care of her father. But then most of her cooking had involved opening up a can of soup or reheating something the women's group from church had dropped off. Anytime she had ventured into combining two or more ingredients, her father had done nothing but complain and accuse her of trying to poison him. She had given up on cooking, until she met

Matt. Her improvement was slow, but she was getting better with practice. Maybe, with Matt's help, there was hope for her when it came to computers too. And who better to teach her? "Are you offering your services along with your equipment?"

"Sure am." He headed for his office. "Come on, let's get started."

Blue entered the office with trepidation. She had only been in there a couple of times since moving into Matt's house. Once to vacuum the rug, and once to dust. There was something intimidating about dark screens and silent keyboards. They seemed to be waiting for someone to flip a switch so they could come alive. Some people believed computers would rule the world someday. She was one of them. They already controlled just about everything in a person's life. From a car's ignition, to checkouts at supermarkets, they were everywhere. They knew who you were, what you did and how much money you made. They probably knew a person's hidden talents, if he failed to return a library book, and what kind of toothpaste he used. It was alarming to sit down in front of one and expect it to follow your command.

Matt walked to the side of the room, where a simple desktop computer sat on a table. "Here, this is the easiest one to use."

She looked at the computer and smiled. It looked remarkably like the ones she'd used in numerous computer labs. "This one should be fine."

Matt pulled out a chair. "Sit." After she sat he

pulled over the chair from behind his desk and joined her. "All you need to know is how to use a mouse." He pushed the beige plastic mouse in front of her and turned on the machine. "It's all point and click, point and click."

An hour later Blue laughed as she maneuvered her way along the superhighway. Who would have thought traveling the Internet could be so easy? She glanced at the man beside her and grinned. "Oh, Matt, how can I ever thank you?"

"You just did." He nodded toward the screen highlighting the NFL and the scores from the regular season's first games. "Is there anyplace else you want to visit before logging off?"

She shook her head. "There are just too many places to visit. How do you ever get any real work done?"

"Sometimes it's not easy, but I've been working with computers for so long, it's not like walking into a candy shop and being told to sample everything and that none of it will make you fat."

She chuckled. She had noticed that the candy dish in the living room had suffered quite a few onslaughts since his return. Matt must have a sweet tooth. "Tell me again how to log off."

He showed her a few simple point-and-clicks, and within seconds the computer screen was once again blank. "That's all there is to it."

She stood up and stretched. "You really don't mind me using it?"

"If I minded I wouldn't have offered." He used the table as leverage and stood up. "Feel free to use it anytime."

On impulse she threw her arms around him and hugged him hard. "Thanks." Not only was he allowing her to use the computer, but he hadn't treated her like some idiot for not knowing what surely had to be basics. His patience and time had been greatly appreciated.

After a moment of hesitation, he returned the embrace. Through her cotton T-shirt she could feel his hands caress her back and she nestled deeper into his arms. This was where she wanted to be. His heart thundering within his chest matched the rapid pace of her own. Matt was feeling it too.

She lifted her head and silently issued him an invitation. Groaning, he accepted with a heated kiss that melted her knees and her senses. This time she wanted it all. She wanted to feel Matt.

Without breaking the kiss, she grabbed the bottom of his shirt and pulled it up. It was halfway up his chest before Matt broke the kiss and helped her by taking it off the rest of the way.

With a trembling hand she caressed the chestnut curls covering his chest. They felt like down sprouting from muscular steel. Hot steel. Her tongue moistened her lips as she stared at the curls floating through her fingers. She leaned forward and gently placed a kiss on each of his protruding nipples. Desire rushed through her body when she stepped back and noticed the effect the two simple kisses had on him.

He dragged in a harsh breath. "They work the same way yours do."

She saw the hungry look darkening his eyes. "Does it feel as good?" She could still remember the heat that had flared in the pit of her stomach when he'd tenderly suckled her breasts.

"Heaven doesn't even begin to describe it." He grabbed the hem of her shirt and pulled it over her head in one fluid motion. His gaze met hers as he undid the front clasp of her bra. "You describe it."

She watched enthralled as his mouth sucked in the exposed tip of her breast. His tongue flicked over the hardened nipple, and she grabbed his arms and threw back her head. He placed one last kiss on her breast and moved to lavish the other nipple with the same treatment.

With great reluctance, he ended the torment and raised his head. "Well, how does it feel?"

Blue shrugged her shoulders and allowed the bra to drop to the floor. "Heavenly is as close as I can come." She stood on her toes, encircled his neck with her arms, and brought her lips to within inches of his. "Simply heavenly."

He captured her teasing mouth with a ravishing kiss. Her breasts were crushed against his hard chest. This was what she missed the other night. The feel of Matt. She rubbed her chest against his and felt his arms tighten around her.

The kiss deepened. Tongues mated. Heat erupted into a fiery volcano of need. Blue felt moisture gather at the juncture of her thighs as his arousal pressed against her. Matt's hands slid down to cup her bottom just as the phone rang.

He glared at the offending instrument for a second before turning back to her. "Let it ring. If it's important, they'll call back."

She had to agree with his logic and immediately recaptured his mouth. On the seventh ring, though, she conceded defeat and broke the kiss. "I think you should answer it. It sounds important."

"How could a ring sound important?"

"Please . . ." It was probably some salesman selling cemetery plots or subscriptions to magazines, but whoever it was wasn't giving up easily.

Matt released her, grabbed the phone in the middle of the ninth ring, and barked, "Hello."

Blue smiled at his displeasure but self-consciously picked up her T-shirt and slipped it over her head. She was more than willing to pick up where they had been interrupted, but she wasn't standing around topless while Matt haggled with a salesman. She watched as he ran a hand through his messed-up hair and muttered, "Yeah, this is he."

Her smile slipped as his attention left her and focused on the caller. She listened to the one-sided conversation that consisted of "When?", "How long ago?", a series of "damns," a spiel of high-tech jargon that she couldn't make heads or tails of, and mention of a flight.

Matt slowly replaced the receiver and glanced at the clock. "Oh, hell."

"What's wrong, Matt?"

He gave her a smile that didn't quite reach his eyes. "I have to leave immediately for Wichita."

"Kansas?"

"Unless you know of another Wichita."

Frustration and confusion crept through her. She didn't want Matt going anywhere tonight. They had been so close. Obviously, whatever the phone call had been about, it was important. "When do you leave?"

"I have just enough time to throw a few things into a suitcase. Would you drive me to the airport in Albany?"

She gave him what she hoped was an understanding smile. "Sure."

He walked over to her and cupped her chin, forcing her to look him in the eyes. "I have to go, Blue. Believe me, I don't want to, but I have to. It's an emergency at their general hospital. I helped set up the data entry program, and now after months in operation it's gone completely down. No one out there can figure out what went wrong." He brushed a curl away from her cheek. "Without the program they can't retrieve information on their patients."

She felt tears build up behind her eyes and rapidly blinked them away. Patients could become sicker, if not worse, unless Matt left immediately. She knew that and understood. So why was it hurting so bad? "It's okay, Matt. If you want I'll even help you pack."

Hunger flared in his eyes as he stared at her mouth. He traced her lower lip with his thumb. "I believe we have something very special here, Blue. I would give my right arm not to leave, but I think neither one of us could live with the consequences."

"I don't like it either, Matt." She took a deep breath and gave him a winning smile. "But I do understand."

He brushed a kiss across her mouth. "Will you miss me?"

"Terribly." She reached behind her and picked up his shirt from where she had dropped it on the table. "There'll be plenty of time when you get back." She didn't need to explain time for what. By the fire in Matt's eyes, he understood completely.

"Nothing and no one could keep me in Wichita one minute longer than necessary." He reached for his crutch. "Give me five minutes to take a quick shower before helping me pack." He winked as he headed for the door. "Maybe by then I'll have the control I need to not miss my flight when we're in the same bedroom."

SEVEN

Twenty-four hours later Matt inserted his key into the door of his hotel room and yawned. Going over thirty-six hours without sleep was playing havoc with his mind. Figures on the screens had blurred, commands had no longer made sense, and a person could only drink so much coffee.

He removed his jacket and sat on the edge of the bed. With a weary sigh he flopped back across the mattress and closed his eyes. He thought of Blue and wondered what she was doing back at home. *Home!* It had such a nice ring to it. For years the beautiful log house had been only that, a house. Now it felt like a home. And he missed it, but not nearly as much as he missed Blue. In just a minute he was going to pick up the phone and call her. All he needed was two minutes to rest his eyes and get all his thoughts going in the same direction.

❖━━━━━━━❖

Blue sprinted into the kitchen and picked up the phone in the middle of the second ring. "Hello." She was hoping it was Matt. When she'd arrived home from a day of waiting on tables and classes, she had discovered a bouquet of wildflowers sitting on the porch. A local florist had delivered the flowers and a short note: *Call you tonight, Matt.*

"Blue?"

"Who else would be answering your phone?"

"It didn't sound like you at first."

"Sorry." She wasn't about to admit being out of breath from her mad dash across the living room. "Thank you for the flowers, Matt, they're lovely. How did you know I love wildflowers?"

"Just a lucky guess." His soft laughter touched her heart. "How was your day?"

She twisted the white cord around her finger. She wanted to tell him how much she had missed him. "The same as yesterday. Got up at five to work the breakfast shift at Jack's, went to classes all day, and came home with a pile of homework." She laughed good-naturedly. She had known what she was getting into when she'd registered at Bennington and didn't have one regret. The part she hadn't counted on, though, was coming home to an empty house. It had never bothered her before. "How's it going down there?"

"As well as can be expected. I got the system up by bypassing a bunch of commands. The hospital can now retrieve vital information, but they can't enter any until I figure out what happened."

"Have any ideas?"

His voice dropped to a rough murmur that caressed her senses. "I've got hundreds of ideas."

She grinned. "Are we still talking about computers?"

"Nope."

Her grin widened. "Good."

Four days later Blue found herself rushing around like a madwoman about to embark on the Crusades. Matt was coming home. He had called every night since that first phone call. Each call had gotten progressively longer and hotter. By the time they had whispered their good nights, she had been ready to claw wallpaper off the wall with her fingernails. Frustration didn't begin to describe how she felt. She had even gone as far as sleeping in Matt's bed at night just to feel a little closer to him.

That morning she had gotten up at five-thirty to clean. She had changed sheets, dusted, vacuumed, and put a roast in the Crock-Pot, following every one of Jack's instructions to the letter. Before rushing out the door for classes, she had stacked logs in the fireplace, ready to be lit. All she had to do was set a match to the decorative pile, and presto—instant romance.

When Matt had called the night before and explained that Jared was picking him up at the airport and that he'd be home for dinner, she had been so excited. She had his homecoming planned to the last detail. Firelight, soft music, and a good home-cooked meal. Timing was the key element. She had to rush from school to the post office before they closed, stop at the store to pick up a bottle of wine, then dash home. As soon as she got home, she had to check on the roast, light the fire, take a quick shower, and dress in the outfit she'd already laid out across Matt's bed. It sounded so simple. So easy. An idiot could have done it blindfolded.

Blue stood in the living room and glared at the fireplace, amazed that such a totally organized plan could go to hell so fast. School was a foggy blur, and Matt's mail was lying on the floor of the Bronco drenched in wine. How was she to know that in the state of Vermont they allowed idiots to drive? Some jerk had pulled out in front of her, and if it hadn't been for her seat belt and quick reactions, she would have ended up in the same condition as the wine—smashed. As it was, the only damage was one broken bottle of wine, soaked mail, and the once spotless green carpeting on the passenger side of the Bronco would never be the same.

Determined that nothing else would ruin Matt's homecoming, she had continued home. One look at the congealed mess permanently adhered to the inside of the Crock-Pot had almost gotten the best of her. A quick look into the freezer had netted frozen fish sticks and potato tots.

She had given herself a pep talk as she'd headed

for the next step, lighting the fire. She'd knelt on the hearth and put a lit match to some newspaper she had stuffed under the logs. The paper went up in a blaze, fizzled out into a cloud of black smoke, and nothing. No roaring fire. No instant romance. Okay, if it wanted to be stubborn, so could she. She grabbed another handful of newspaper and headed back to the fireplace. As she crumpled and jammed the paper into every available space, a smile crossed her lips. This was going to be the most romantic fire Matt had ever seen, and she'd be waiting in front of it for him.

Blue burned her finger on the third match, but she finally managed to light the paper. Black smoke billowed out of the fireplace to sting her eyes. Tears trickled down her cheeks as she desperately tried to find the damper handle. Why hadn't she thought of that before she lit the paper! If the damper wasn't open, there would be no place for the smoke to go.

She was so preoccupied with trying to locate the handle, she didn't hear Matt and Jared pull up out front. The sound of their approaching footsteps was muffled by the curses tumbling from her lips.

Matt and Jared entered the house and froze in utter amazement at the sight that greeted them. His eyes instantly stinging from the smoke, Matt stared at Blue standing totally dejected in front of a smoldering fire. A trail of tears ran down her blackened cheeks, a finger, that he guessed was burned, was jammed into her mouth. She was wearing worn jeans, an old T-shirt streaked with soot, and sneakers with holes in them.

He dropped his crutch, limped across the room to stand in front of her, and opened his arms. The impact of her throwing herself against his chest nearly sent them both to the floor. She had never felt so good.

Jared placed Matt's suitcase by the door and walked past them to the fireplace. He reached up inside the chimney and opened the damper. Smiling with amusement, he headed for the patio doors and slid one open so that the smoke had somewhere to go. He caught the silent thank you in Matt's eyes, nodded, and left.

Matt placed a kiss on the golden curls nestled under his chin and murmured soothing words to the bawling woman in his arms. What was he going to do with Blue?

Love her! was the immediate response from both his body and his mind. For six days and five frustrating nights he had done nothing but think of her. His thoughts were a jumble of emotional vines. His life had turned into a Bob Dylan song. He was tangled up in Blue.

He eased himself and Blue onto the couch. The fire in the fireplace was dying, leaving behind black crinkly burned paper and logs that were barely scorched. Blue's fire hadn't caught. It was just as well. Considering the amount of wood she'd used, they would have been forced out of the house by the heat.

When she gave a dainty sniffle and her tears seemed to be slowing, he asked, "Are you okay now?"

She reached for a tissue from the box on the end table and blew her nose. "Sure, I'm fine. Nothing else is, but I am." She grabbed another tissue and wiped her eyes. She gave him a watery smile and threw herself back into his arms. "I've missed you."

He chuckled as he held her tight. "Not as much as I've missed you." Here he sat with a woman who looked like she had just escaped the towering inferno and he was fully and achingly aroused. He had been walking around semiaroused since the night they had parked on top of Elk Mountain and she had shattered in his arms. Now she was once again in his arms and his body was screaming for release.

She unburied her face from the collar of his white shirt and groaned. "Oh, my gosh!" He glanced down at the black smudges where her face had touched him. She pulled back in horror and asked, "Am I really that bad?"

He cupped both her cheeks in his hands. "Your face is black, your eyes are bloodshot. . . ." He smiled at her look of disgust. "And I've never seen you look lovelier." He brought her face closer and captured her lips with a caress as gentle as the summer rain.

The kiss immediately flared into something more potent. Something hot and needy. He reluctantly ended it before it consumed them both and placed a few needed inches between them. "What was the fire for?"

"You." She grabbed another tissue and rubbed at her face. "I wanted everything perfect for you when you came home." Tears threatened to fall again as she glanced around the nearly smoke-free living room. "I had dinner cooking all day. Jack gave me the recipe. It was supposed to be foolproof, but something must be wrong with your Crock-Pot because whatever's in it is totally inedible." She sniffled again. "Some idiot pulled out in front of me on my way home and the wine that I bought to go with dinner smashed onto the Bronco floor *and* on top of your mail." Her lip started to tremble and her voice rose a notch. "I was supposed to take a shower, get all dressed up, and be waiting in front of a roaring fire for you when you walked through the door."

He traced her lower lip with his thumb. "You were waiting in front of a roaring fire when I walked through the door." He placed a light teasing kiss on the end of her nose where he knew a scattering of freckles was buried under the soot. "Why don't you go up and take that shower now? After you're cleaned up we'll see about dinner."

"There're fish sticks and potato tots in the freezer." She swiped her nose, where he'd kissed, and saw the back of her hand was now streaked with soot. She wiped her hand on her jeans. "I'll be down in a little while."

He watched her mount the stairs with a slight

stoop to her shoulders. Poor Blue. She had tried so hard to have everything perfect for him. He grimaced as he noticed the front of his shirt was streaked with soot and tears. Blue's tears. Lord, he felt like a heel. Here she had been busting her rear to make everything special for his homecoming, while he had done nothing more strenuous than sit on a plane and fantasize about all the different ways he wanted to make love to her.

He should be shot. He should be horsewhipped. He glanced at his shirt one more time. Hell, he should go take a shower and change before she saw what she had done to his shirt and started crying again. He rose from the couch and hobbled to his crutch. He was getting pretty good at short distances without the aid of the one crutch, but he still needed the support to make it up the stairs.

He gave his suitcase a glance as he headed for the stairs. There was nothing in it that he needed right away. He'd carry it up later.

As he entered his bedroom the sound of his shower being turned on stopped him in his tracks. His gaze landed on the silky teal-colored outfit laid neatly across his bed. Blue's outfit. His gaze swung back to the closed bathroom door. Blue was taking a shower in his bathroom, not hers. His mind quickly added two and two and came up with the conclusion that Blue would be spending her nights in his bed from now on.

He grinned as he started to unbutton his shirt.

❖━━━━━❖

Blue had just rinsed the last of the shampoo from her hair when the shower door opened. She batted a clump of wet hair out of her eyes and watched as Matt stepped into the large shower stall. Trying to suck in some much-needed air, she ended up with a mouthful of water. Lord, he was beautiful. From his devilish grin, to his scrumptious chest, to his maleness standing in full glory. A fiery flush swept up her cheeks as her gaze flew back up to his.

He shrugged, obviously amused. "Sorry. There're some reactions a male can't hide."

"That's okay." Her voice sounded squeaky and weak to her own ears. She forced herself to relax. So what if this was the first time a man had seen her totally naked. It shouldn't matter that she probably resembled a drowned rat. It would be downright impossible to look seductive while standing under a downpour. She was, after all, the one who'd invited herself into his shower and bedroom. Matt, being the gentleman that he was, had only taken her up on her invitation. She was thankful that he had. She would have been totally humiliated if he hadn't.

He held out his hand, glancing at the bar of soap she was holding. "I've dreamed about washing your back."

His grin told her that wasn't all he had dreamed about. She handed him the soap and turned her back to him. Large hands slid up her spine as warm water cascaded down her breasts. She closed her eyes and raised her face toward the spray as new sensations churned through her body. Matt's strong hands gently massaged the length of her back and down over her hips to lightly squeeze her bottom.

A kiss skimmed the nape of her neck as he moved closer. She felt his chest rub her shoulder blades as his arousal nudged her lower back. She bit her lip to keep from smiling. "What are you doing?"

He moved closer. "Saving on soap."

This time she couldn't prevent the laugh that escaped her as she leaned against him. Teeth gently nipped at her earlobe as he rubbed lather onto her stomach. A purr of pleasure vibrated in the back of her throat as his hands slowly moved higher.

Half turning in his arms, she sought his lips. Desire raced through her veins as she heard him groan, and she slipped her tongue into his mouth.

Water poured down over her head as the kiss grew more passionate and Matt dropped the soap. His hands had something else to hold on to. Her. She enthusiastically returned the gesture. His skin was slick with water and hot with desire. Her fingers smoothed their way down his chest toward his straining manhood.

With a muttered curse, Matt broke the kiss, turned off the water, and opened the shower door. Tugging on her hand, he carefully pulled her from the stall. "There's no way we would survive what I want to do in that death trap." He took two towels, wrapped one around his waist, and started to dry her with the other.

Blue had never felt so pampered or frustrated in her whole life. She wanted Matt, and she wanted him now. The thick towel was absorbing every bead of moisture on her back. As soon as Matt rubbed the towel lower, water would drip from her hair, and he would have to start the whole procedure over again.

Frustrated at the amount of time he was spending on her back, she reached past him, grabbed another towel, and ruthlessly rubbed her hair. She peeked out from underneath the unruly damp curls and saw Matt smiling at her. She shrugged. "We would have been here all night."

"I wouldn't have complained." He carefully patted the few remaining drops that glistened on her face.

She sucked in a breath as the towel slid down her throat toward her breasts. She could feel her nipples harden in anticipation of his touch. With trembling fingers she untucked the towel wrapped around his waist. When all he did was raise an eyebrow, she grinned. "Fair is fair." She stretched up onto her toes and started to dry his hair.

He laughed, rubbed his face into the towel she was holding, and knelt in front of her.

Blue felt the warmth of his breath bathe her nipples and slowly lowered her arms. His mouth was a hairbreadth away from her breasts. She watched as he puckered his lips and the dusky peaks seemed to gravitate toward him. She nearly fainted with pleasure as he gently pulled one nipple into his mouth. The towel she had been using slipped from her fingers and tumbled to the floor.

With exquisite tenderness he continued to move his towel over her hips and down her thighs and legs, all the while bathing the tips of her breasts with his tongue. The pull of his mouth started a yearning deep inside her. A yearning only he could quench.

Blue bit her lip as Matt released her nipple and trailed his mouth down her stomach. He captured with his tongue a lone drop of moisture that was beaded in her belly button. She felt his warm hands cup her buttocks as he trailed a line of kisses from her navel to the mound of damp curls guarding her womanhood. A hoarse plea escaped her as her hand clutched his hair in a futile attempt to bring him closer.

He raised his head and glanced around the bathroom. Standing slowly, he held out a hand toward her. "I won't make love to you for the first time in the bathroom, Blue." He glanced at the shower and grinned. "Give me time for my leg to heal and we'll try it later."

Her gaze followed his to the steamed shower stall. She couldn't think of one reason why they shouldn't try to be more adventurous once his leg had healed properly. Something about warm water and hotter hands had been very exciting, to say the least. "You got yourself a deal."

Together they left the bathroom and walked into his bedroom. Her eyebrows rose when she saw that the blankets on the king-size bed had been turned down and that her clothes had been moved to a chair. She glanced at Matt, and he smiled sheepishly.

"A man can hope, can't he?" he said.

She reached up and placed a kiss on his chin. "Show me what else a man can do."

Matt didn't need a second invitation. He lay down across the bed, bringing her with him. His mouth seized her willing lips and she melted onto his hardness.

Blue could feel his muscles tremble beneath her weight and gloried in the knowledge that she was the cause. Her hands caressed his chest, his sides, his hips. She couldn't get enough of him. She wanted to touch him everywhere. Her fingers slid lower. She heard his harsh indrawn breath as she encircled his throbbing maleness.

Smoothness. It wasn't what she had expected. If someone had asked her what she expected a man to feel like, smoothness would not have entered her mind. It wasn't an unpleasant feeling. As a matter of fact it was quite nice—smooth, hard, warm, and vibrating with life.

She was just about to explore further when Matt captured her roaming hands. He turned her, so she was lying flat on her back, with both of her hands pinned against the pillow beneath her head. "I'll let you explore to your heart's content some other time, but not right now. A man can only take so much pleasure, and then it's over before it has a chance to begin."

She grinned with understanding. The man who felt like sun-warmed stone in her hands had a breaking point. She was eager to see what could break Matthew Stone apart.

Seeing the gleam in her eye, he shook his head and whispered, "Now let's see how much pleasure you can handle." He released her hands and trailed one finger across her moist lips. When her tongue came out to meet his finger, he laughed and slid his finger down her throat.

She groaned as he circled first one nipple, then the other. "Matt . . ."

"Shhh." His lips followed his finger. "Let me do this my way, Blue. I don't want to hurt you."

The concern in his voice touched her heart. "You could never hurt me, Matt."

He placed another kiss on the tips of her breasts. "Never deliberately, Blue, but this is your first time." He lightly caressed her trembling thighs. She relaxed her legs as his fingers stroked higher. Ever-nearer. She arched her hips and was rewarded with pleasure as his fingers slowly entered her.

"You're ready for me?"

She heard the wonderment in his voice and reached out to cradle his head. "I've *been* ready for you. Haven't you figured that out by now?"

Surprise, joy, and hunger flared in his eyes as he

prepared himself to enter her. He whispered her name, then kissed her as he entered her.

His mouth absorbed her cry of shock. And his swift invasion of her body was more of a shock than the pain she had been expecting.

Matt didn't move, except to raise his head. "Are you okay?"

Blue lay perfectly still herself and wondered if she was okay. The shock and discomfort had only lasted a moment. Now she felt a fullness. Matt's fullness. She forced her thighs to relax and felt Matt move in deeper. She smiled.

"Blue?"

She lifted her hips and wrapped her legs around the back of his thighs. She could now feel the entire length of his hardness nestled deep within her. A groan rumbled somewhere deep within his chest. Blue purred and arched her back again. "I'm fine, Matt."

He studied her face, looking, she was sure, for signs of discomfort. When a smile broke across his strained face, she returned it with one of her own. "You're more than fine." He kissed the tip of her nose. "You're beautiful."

With small movements he started their dance of love. She matched his rhythm thrust for thrust and breath for breath. Nothing she had ever experienced had felt like this. The pleasure Matt had shown her the other night was nothing compared with what she was experiencing now. The tempo increased and the rhythm became wild, but still she held on. She had to discover where Matt was taking her as they climbed higher, higher, faster. . . .

Together they reached the top and she knew she was about to topple over the edge. She wanted Matt with her. She needed him with her this time.

She held on to him as the abyss opened up and she shattered into a million pieces. His name was torn from her throat. "Matt!" In the dim recesses of her mind she heard his shout as he followed her.

Matt held Blue tight against his side and felt her lips form a smile against his chest. "What's so funny?" He barely had the energy to talk. Never had he experienced anything as powerful or as wonderful as what had just happened. He wondered if Blue had experienced the same emotions. He wondered how she couldn't have.

She raised her head. "Nothing's funny. Everything is wonderful."

"No regrets?"

Her smile faded slightly. "Just one."

His heart slammed against his chest. "What's that?"

She giggled. "That it hadn't happened sooner."

With a quick move, he had her pinned beneath him. The little witch! She had nearly given him heart failure. "Welcome home, Mr. Stone," she said, laughing harder.

He cocked one eyebrow as desire rekindled

throughout his body. How could he want her again so soon? "Mr. Stone, is it?"

She pressed her hips against his. "As in, 'hard as . . .'" She rubbed against him again, leaving him in no doubt about what she was referring to.

"Blue, we can't."

She ran her hand down his back and playfully swatted his backside. "Can't?"

He closed his eyes and prayed for strength. He shouldn't make love to her again tonight. It was too soon. If he were a true gentleman, he'd get up and take a cold shower and give her some time. "We shouldn't."

She reached up and brought his head down to her waiting lips. "Please make love to me again, Matt."

One glance at those moist, pleading lips and he knew he had lost the battle. With a muffled groan he captured her mouth. Once again the journey had started.

EIGHT

Matt stood behind Blue's chair and nibbled on the back of her neck as the last of her report, "The Adverse Effects of Television on Preschoolers," printed out. The previous Saturday morning he had helped her gather data for the report by viewing ten children's programs with her and counting each incident of physical or verbal abuse. He had been appalled at the numbers while Blue had assured him that if even a small percentage of children practiced what they saw, the world would be filled with six-year-old serial killers and total chaos. Which it was not.

Blue's next report was going to be on the different effects, if there were any, of cartoon characters acting abusively and violently, and shows in which real people acted out the parts. He thought it was a fascinating subject, but he was more fascinated by Blue's concern and interest in children.

Blue was planning a career where she would be working with children on a daily basis. It had to mean, at the very least, that she liked children. Didn't it? Why else would she be getting her degree in early childhood education? It was a respectable and admirable career. It was also a stable career. Something that was at total odds with Blue's current lifestyle. In the past two years she had lived in five states and had held a total of sixteen different jobs.

Even his mother had a better track record than that. For the past eighteen months his mother had stayed put in Tranquility selling her crystals and herbs. Her little shop wasn't setting any sales records, but it supported her, and more important, she seemed to be happy and content. He wondered if Blue would ever be happy and content if she stopped her traveling ways. Was she living like this because it was the only way she knew how to put herself through college, or did she enjoy the endless towns and continuous parade of strangers? Or, was she running from something?

His mother had started her nomadic lifestyle after the death of her husband, his father. Blue had started hers soon after her own father's death. Was it a coincidence, or were the two women more alike than he wanted to believe?

His lips skimmed to where he knew there was a sensitive area behind her ear. For the past two weeks he had used every free moment Blue had to learn and enjoy each inch of her luscious body. It had been the best two weeks of his life. He never wanted it to end.

"Matt?"

"Hmmm . . ." Golden curls tickled his nose and he could detect the slight flowery scent of the perfume she had applied that morning.

"It's done printing." Her voice held a hint of laughter as she slid out of the chair and grabbed for the pages.

"Good." He nabbed her around the waist and hauled her back against his chest. "Remind me to buy a faster printer." His mouth found the moist spot he had been nibbling on a moment before.

Blue allowed the papers to slip from her fingers onto the keyboard as she leaned farther into his embrace. "Maybe you should try eating more dinner."

He smiled against the silky skin of her neck. "That's not what I'm hungry for and you know it." He refused to comment on her current attempt at making meatballs and spaghetti. At least it had been edible, and if the lead weight lying in his stomach was any indication, it also was filling. Blue's culinary skills were improving daily. So were her computer skills.

She no longer waited until he was around to boot up the computer he had said she could use. She felt quite comfortable sitting at the keyboard, and was no longer intimidated about commanding bits and bytes to do her will. During the past several days he'd begun to fear he might have created a monster. A monster who was relishing her daily fix of cyberspace.

She remained in his arms a moment longer, then moved away. "Well, you're going to have to give me a couple more minutes." She picked up the pages she had dropped. "I need to get these in order and then into a folder. It's due tomorrow morning."

Matt leaned against his desk, watching her. He could see the light gleaming in her eyes that told him she knew the report was "A" material. Blue poured one hundred percent of herself into her schoolwork, just like everything else she did.

The other morning he had surprised her by showing up at Jack's Diner for breakfast with Jared and his wife, Alison. Blue had hustled and bustled from one table to the next taking orders, filling empty coffee cups, and delivering plates overflowing with food. All with a friendly smile. In the short amount of time she had lived in Greenhaven and worked at Jack's, she had learned half the town's population, greeting the majority of customers by name. It had unsettled him, seeing how quickly and easily she had settled in. Would her leaving be just as quick and easy?

"So, beautiful," he said, "what are you planning on doing with all this knowledge once you graduate?"

She checked the page numbers one last time before using the three-hole punch. "I'm more worried about graduating at the end of May than what I'll be doing come June."

"Your grades are fine. Why the worry?"

"This semester should be fine." She glanced at his injured leg. "You're improving much faster than you had originally thought."

"The doctor still hasn't signed off on allowing me to drive yet." He didn't like the direction this conversation was heading. "I use the cane now instead of the crutch, because it's easier and less cumbersome. I still need you, Blue."

She gnawed at her lower lip before returning her attention to the folder in her hands. "But for how long?"

"The deal was until the end of the semester." He wanted to tell her he would always need her, but something stopped him. That something was fear. The fear that Blue didn't need him and that one morning he would awaken to find her gone. His instincts told him she would stay until the end of the semester, because he needed her. Blue, by nature, was a nurturer. Not only had she cared for her ailing father for years, she stayed with Matt himself when he needed her, and even her chosen career pointed in that direction. He didn't want her caring ways, though. He wanted her heart.

He had fallen in love with Blue. There was no other way to describe his feelings toward her. He had fallen in love with the wrong type of woman, and no matter how much his head argued against such emotion, his heart refused to listen. He was in love with a woman who, in all likelihood, would be gone by Christmas. Unless he did something. The question was, what? He had absolutely no idea what would make Blue stay. The key to understanding her was in her past.

He gazed at her bent head as she neatly printed the title of the report on the outside of the folder. She had the face of an angel and a body luscious enough to tempt the devil himself. Somewhere deep inside her heart and mind was the answer.

Matt folded his arms to keep from reaching for her. If he touched her now they would end up in bed and he would still be searching for answers. Satisfied physically but not mentally. Tonight he wanted some answers. "I was curious as to what kind of job you'll be looking for after you receive your degree. Are you planning on teaching on the elementary level?"

"I'm not counting on it. There aren't a whole lot of openings out there for teachers."

"So why major in children's education if you can't get a job in that field?"

"Because it's what I want to do, and who said being an elementary-school teacher is the only job out there? There are hundreds of jobs for which having a degree in early childhood education would be a benefit."

"You have something else in mind?"

She grinned. "Could be."

Her smile said it all. Beulah Crawford was a woman with a plan. He wondered if there was room for him in it. "Care to elaborate?"

She shrugged. "It's only a silly dream."

"No dreams are silly and this"—he swept his arms out, indicating his office and all the computers—"was once a dream."

"You're right. Dreams aren't silly." She carefully stacked her notes and the report into a neat pile. "I want to open my own preschool."

"Really?"

She gave him a curious look. "Why would I lie about something like that?"

"I didn't mean it like that. I think opening your own preschool sounds wonderful." If she was planning on starting her own school, wouldn't that mean she was planning on staying in one place? He wondered what the chances were that he could convince her to open her school right here in Greenhaven.

"You think it's wonderful?" she repeated.

"Sure. You'll make a fantastic teacher and you love children."

One of her eyebrows rose at that comment. "How would you know if I love children or not?"

He grinned. "I've seen the way you fuss and play with the kids who are in the waiting room at the doctor's office." His weekly doctor's appointments had been very enlightening where Blue was concerned. Living on the mountain didn't give him a chance to see her interact with other people, especially children. He had had the one chance to observe her at the diner, and she had proven his suspicions correct. Blue was a people person. But nothing lit up her face as the children in the waiting room at his doctor's did.

"Everyone makes a fuss over children," she said.

"No, everyone makes a fuss over babies and toddlers. Not everyone appreciates children once they pass the cute toddler stage."

"All children are cute no matter what stage they're in."

His grin widened. "See, you love them all." He was surprised by the flush staining her cheeks. What was she embarrassed about? There was nothing wrong with loving children. In fact, the world could do with more people loving children. Then maybe there would be less violence and abuse toward them. "There is one thing I am curious about," he said.

"What's that?"

"Why don't you have a bunch of kids of your own?" He was eternally grateful that she hadn't found herself another man and started a family yet. But he wondered why she hadn't. Blue was a natural-born mother. Didn't she want a family of her own? Or was she too busy running?

Blue stared at Matt as if he had just lost his mind. Why in the world would he want her to have a bunch of kids? she wondered. She didn't want to talk about babies, cute toddlers, or older children. "In case it slipped your attention, I'm not married."

"That's not what I meant, Blue."

"What exactly did you mean, then?" She would have never classed Matt in the same category as her father, but maybe deep down inside all men were the same. "Just because the woman has the womb, Matt, doesn't mean she wants to use it. For years I listened to my father harp on me to 'settle down, get married, and bear me some grandchildren.'" Years of emotional abuse caused her voice to tremble with buried rage. "I would never bring a baby into this world just because someone wanted a grandchild. And I refuse to marry because it was the *thing to do* back in Iowa. And I could never figure out what exactly I was supposed to be settling down from. My wild youth consisted of taking care of my father, going to school for a short time, and on a rare occasion, sneaking over to Caleb's barn, hopping on my motorcycle, and allowing the wind and the road to ease my worries for an hour or two."

Matt raised his hands in surrender. "Whoa, where did all that come from? All I wanted to know is if you ever thought about having children of your own."

Blue looked away from the confusion clouding Matt's eyes. It wasn't his fault that he didn't understand. She didn't understand it herself. Half the time she thought about a family of her own, and the other half she knew it would never be. A family's love was an illusion portrayed in books and on television. It wasn't real. "I'm not going to have any children, Matt."

"Why not?"

"Because I'd probably fail at being a mother."

"That's ridiculous, Blue. Whoever filled your head with such utter nonsense?"

She gave him a ghost of a smile and the truth. "My father." If she had met Matt when she was younger, when she still believed in fairy tales and happily-ever-afters, he would have been her hero. As it was, Caleb had been the closest thing to a hero she had seen and she had never once gotten to go to the ball. Caleb had understood what she had been going through. Problem was, he'd been going through some rough times of his own and neither one of them had had any answers.

"Your father?" Matt repeated. "I thought you said he wanted you to have children."

"He wanted me to have children, because he believed that was what a woman did. She took care of the house, cooked meals, and bore children. He proclaimed me a total failure when it came to taking care of the house."

"That's not true. Look how well you've taken care of this house."

"I haven't run the vacuum all week, there's a coat of dust on just about everything, and I won't even mention how I turned your underwear and socks pink."

"It wasn't your fault that you didn't see that red T-shirt left in the washer."

She pretended not to hear him. She knew she wasn't Susie Homemaker. "He declared a dozen times a week that I was trying to poison him."

"Your cooking isn't *that* bad. I don't expect you

to serve five-course dinners every night. You do go to school and have a part-time job. Lord, Blue, you're only human."

This time her smile was more genuine. Why hadn't she met Matt when she was eighteen? Maybe then she would have had the strength to stand up to her father once in a while instead of listening to his complaints and lectures hour after hour, day after day, year after year. The endless preaching about morals and sins of the flesh. The contradictions in everything he said.

"Make me dinner, girl." "What's this slop, are you trying to poison me again?" "Why aren't you married and having babies like a normal woman?" "What man will want you if you always have your nose in some book?" She had long ago stopped trying to figure out what was right and what was wrong. She had been spun in so many circles, she didn't know where her father's thoughts ended and her own thoughts began.

The day they had lowered Neville Crawford into the ground she had been beyond caring. The last of her family was gone, and she never wanted one again. Her father had drained everything out of her, except her dream of getting an education and making something of herself. She might not ever have a family again, but she was going to have a life. A life she created.

"You're sweet, Matt. But there are some things you just don't understand."

He walked over to her and cupped her face in his hands. "Make me understand, Blue."

She shook her head. How could she make him understand when she didn't understand it herself? She had been torn and battered for so long, she refused to sail down those waters again. "I thought you were happy with me the way I am?"

His voice gentled and his fingers stroked her cheeks. "I'm very happy with you, Blue. I've never been happier in my life than I have been these past several weeks."

She smiled and turned her face to his rough palm. Now that it was too chilly outside to swim and they'd closed the pool, Matt had taken up hiking and woodchopping as forms of exercises. Hiking she could see was helping his leg, but woodchopping was a new one on her. When she had questioned Matt about it, he had only smiled and said she would appreciate it more come cold winter nights.

She closed her eyes and felt his arms slip around her, and wondered how many cold winter nights she would share with Matt. Winter came early in Vermont, but she'd be gone come Christmas. Their deal was till the end of the semester and she wouldn't be staying, at least at Matt's house, any longer. She was still hopeful that the housesitting agency could line her up with something in the area so she could graduate from Bennington come May. Maybe they could still see each other.

She was going to miss him terribly, and her departure was still months away. Blue wrapped her arms around his waist and buried her face against his solid chest. He was the injured one between the two of them, but he felt so stable, so sure of himself. For a moment longer she allowed him to support her. To be her strength. To ease the pain of her past.

"Blue?"

She could hear the concern in his voice and forced herself not to dwell on the past. She had her future and her freedom in front of her. When she had left Iowa, she had made a solemn promise to herself—*Live for today, for tomorrow might never be.* Matt was part of her todays. He was showing her things and making her feel emotions she had never thought to experience. She didn't want to waste one precious moment with him.

She pulled back and smiled up at his worried expression. "Do you know what I want to do right this minute?"

"What?" He brushed a curl away from the corner of her eye.

"Make love to you."

His troubled expression lightened considerably with her words. "Now? Here?" There was a rough edge to his voice, but there was also a hint of laughter.

She caressed his chest with one hand while the other pulled his head down to meet her mouth. "Here." Her lips teased the corner of his mouth with a promise of things to come. Her hand slowly slid down his chest, over his hard abdomen, to the front of his jeans. The bulge that greeted her fingers spoke of his desire and need. It matched her own. She sank her teeth into his lower lip and growled, "Now." She didn't want the comfort of his bed or to waste precious minutes climbing a flight of stairs. She wanted him too badly.

Matt glanced at the doorway, his cluttered desk, then at the thick beige carpet on the floor. With a muttered curse, he carefully sank to the floor, taking her with him.

Hours later Matt held Blue in his arms as she slept fitfully. Something he had said that night had disturbed her. Their frantic lovemaking on the office floor had been both exciting and satisfying. But Blue's response had had an unsettling edge to it. She still had the power to make him soar, and she did shatter in his arms, but there'd been something else tonight. Something he couldn't quite put his finger on.

She had been fine all evening, until he'd brought up the topic of babies. Or maybe it was the subject of her career. Then again, she had brought up her father and the twisted abuse he had subjected her to. The choice was endless, and Matt felt guilty for starting the whole thing. All he wanted were some answers on her past. Instead all he got were more questions.

After they had finally managed to get up off the office floor, lock up, and feed the cats, they had headed upstairs. The warm shower they had taken, instead of waking them up, had only helped them to fall asleep as soon as they hit the bed. He had been asleep for an hour when Blue's restlessness woke him. She seemed to settle down once he pulled her into his arms.

It troubled him. Blue usually slept like she was dead and hardly moved throughout the night. Whatever position she fell asleep in was often the position she awoke in. Tonight she had twisted and turned. He had even heard her muttering something in her sleep. He couldn't understand the words, but he had recognized the despair in her voice. Despair he had put there, unknowingly. Despair he wanted to take back, but couldn't. All he could do was hold her and pray that her dreams would be sweet ones.

What kind of man had Neville Crawford been to have hurt his daughter with cruel words and heartless statements? Blue had left a lot unsaid. He had seen it in her face, in the pain that had clouded her eyes. How could a father be so cruel? When he had a daughter, he would treat her like the finest jewel, a little princess, a loving extension of his heart. Because that was what she would be. His son would be treated in the same way. Any children that he had would be conceived in love, born in love, and raised in love.

He frowned as his arms tightened around Blue. She had claimed she didn't want children of her own. Who could blame her, after the way she must have been raised? No wonder she disliked cleaning or cooking. It stood to reason she would balk at motherhood. Having been told all your life that it was the only reason you had been put on this earth was enough to reject it. But how was he to get the family he had always dreamed about if the woman he loved didn't want children?

Blue also didn't seem to want any permanent commitment. She was already talking about leaving at the end of the semester. Had her father really screwed her up that royally that she couldn't handle any sort of commitment? Or did she look on the past couple of months as just a good time? Maybe her heart wasn't involved. Maybe she didn't love him. She had never spoken the words, but that didn't mean much. He had never spoken of the love he felt for her.

He was a coward. He was in love for the first time in his thirty-four years, and he was afraid of telling Blue because he was so unsure about what she felt toward him. He knew she had some affection for him, something more than just a physical attraction. But how deep did her feelings go? Were they deep enough to combat years of abuse from her father? Deep enough to form a commitment? Deep enough to start a family and make his dreams come true?

What about Blue's dreams? Was opening up her own preschool her only dream, or was there another dream? A dream she was afraid even to admit to having?

Matt pulled the comforter up higher and tucked it around Blue's shoulders. The cool autumn air was blowing in through the window he had left cracked open, and he didn't want her catching a chill. She had finally settled down into a restful sleep.

Soft golden curls tickled his chin as he curled up and allowed sleep to take his body and mind. Somehow, someway, he would make Blue see that she had nothing to fear from his love. His future happiness depended on it.

NINE

Blue stood in the middle of the frozen-food section and glared at Matt. He stood in front of her wearing his little boy's smile and clutching a twenty-pound turkey. Thanksgiving was two days away and she had foolishly agreed to take him along when she did the food shopping.

"Don't you think it's a little large for just the two of us?" she asked. The frozen bird looked big enough to feed the entire U.S. Senate.

"I like turkey sandwiches."

"For the rest of your life?" she cried, exasperated at the entire outing. First he'd wanted two different kinds of cranberry sauces, then it had been the paper napkins with pilgrims printed on them. Now he wanted a turkey roughly the size of an emu.

"Please."

She noticed the group of ladies who were gathering by the six-foot display of the Trix bunny advertising his frozen fruit pops. "Matt, I never cooked a raw turkey before." She had once attempted to roast a chicken, but she didn't think Matt would want to hear about that incident. How was she to have known some sadist butcher had bagged the poor bird's heart and other organs and jammed them inside its body cavity?

Looking amused, he asked, "What kind of turkey have you cooked?"

Two more ladies joined the group, causing it to overflow in front of the frozen brussels sprouts. "Fully cooked and frozen," she answered. "It usually comes with a side dish of stuffing, mashed potatoes, and peas and carrots. You pop a few holes in the plastic wrap, throw it into the microwave, hit a few buttons, and presto—turkey." She glanced at their overflowing cart. There should be a law about men being allowed into grocery stores. Soon, Matt would be expecting her to cook everything he had tossed into their cart. "Hey, I have an idea."

"What's that?"

"We can buy a couple of those dinners, open up your cranberries, and we won't have to worry about cooking Thanksgiving dinner." It was what she had done last year for Thanksgiving. The year before that she had stopped off at a Kentucky Fried Chicken and treated herself.

"Don't worry about cooking it, Blue." Matt's smile made her knees go weak. "I've cooked raw turkey before. I'll show you how."

Why did he have to be so handsome and helpful? She couldn't refuse him anything when he smiled that smile. "Okay, but put that one back before you get a hernia. Find a smaller one." She was just turning toward the cart when another thought struck her. "Try to find one already stuffed. That way we won't have to worry about that too."

An hour later Blue carried in the last of the grocery bags and stared in astonishment at the amount of stuff they had bought. Correction, Matt had bought. The man had purchased enough food to feed a third-world country. She had shooed him out of the kitchen after he had made two trips to the Bronco. He was still carrying the cane, but using it sparingly. Soon the cane would be gone and the slight limp he had now would be a thing of the past.

She had noticed his improvement almost daily. At his doctor's appointment earlier that evening, he had been given permission to drive. Matt had driven them from the doctor's office to the store, then home again. Driving was now one more thing he didn't need her to do for him. Soon he wouldn't need her at all. It was a depressing thought.

After all the fuss and complaining about having taken care of her father, one would think she would never want to care for another human being. Even she had thought that, until Matt needed her. For some strange reason, she liked him needing her. She wouldn't like to see Matt permanently disabled or in constant need of assistance. But there were many ways one person needed another. She was beginning to fear that she needed Matt in one of those other ways. She had never felt as alive as she did when she was with him. So energized. So hopeful.

Blue slowly took off her jacket and hung it on the peg near the back door. What did she have to be hopeful about? The semester was almost over; Matt really didn't need her any longer, and never once had he said that he loved her. Not since their little chat in his office about six weeks earlier had any of their conversations become too personal. Which was fine by her. She'd be leaving soon and didn't want to spoil her time left with Matt building arguments. She was too busy building memories.

She glanced around the kitchen and sighed. This was not the kind of memory she wanted of their Thanksgiving together. It was going to take her an hour to find space for all this food. The twenty-pound turkey, which Matt had insisted they buy, would never fit into the freezer. What was she going to do with Wonder Bird?

"Blue?" Matt's voice came from the direction of the living room.

"In here!" She started to pull food out of bags and lay it all on the counter.

Matt entered the kitchen and gave her a strange look. "I hope you weren't looking forward to having a quiet Thanksgiving with just the two of us."

She frowned at a bag of frozen cauliflower and wondered how it had gotten into their cart. She hated cauliflower. "Why?"

"I just listened to my messages."

There was a disturbing tone to Matt's voice that finally penetrated her senses. Something was up. Something he appeared uncertain about saying. He seemed to be searching for words. She slowly placed the bag onto the counter and gave him her full attention. "And . . ."

He glanced at the clock above the stove, then turned back to her. "We have to leave here in forty minutes."

"To go where?"

"The airport."

"The airport?" Now he really was scaring her. "Why are we going to the airport?"

"Because that's where my mother's plane will be landing." He gave her a ghost of a smile that quickly faded. "She left the message when she was at the airport in Chicago, getting a connecting flight from Santa Fe."

Blue felt the walls start to close in on her. "Your mother is coming here?" She glanced at the chaos the kitchen was in and knew the rest of the house wasn't in much better shape. She had been pushing herself at school with the promise that she would do some serious housecleaning during the Thanksgiving break. "Tonight?"

Matt took a couple of steps toward her. "Afraid so. She apologized for the lack of warning, but it was the only flight she could get." He reached out and touched her cheek. "Relax, Blue, it will only be for a few days."

"Days?" Matt's mother was coming for a visit! What in the world was Blue going to do? She couldn't stay there. She had to stay there, she didn't have anywhere else to go. The money she had made working at Jack's was just enough to buy the Chevy she had been eyeing out on Route 7 at some used-car dealership. She needed that car, especially since Matt had just gotten the doctor's blessing to reclaim his Bronco. Sleeping with Matt while his mother was in the house was definitely out. But she couldn't go back to the guest bedroom; his mother would be in there. Maybe she could borrow Matt's sleeping bag and bunk down in the empty third bedroom down the hall. There was nothing in the room but carpeting and an old chair. It would do. It would have to do.

"Now, Blue, don't get all panicky. Veronica's not like most moms."

"Who says I'm panicking?" She wondered what most moms were like. She remembered her own mother, memories from before her eleventh birthday. Somehow she didn't think Matt's mom sewed frilly party dresses or baked chocolate-chip cookies with extra chips, just because Blue liked them that way. Or would go through every bag of M&M's and pick out all the yellow ones so Blue could have her own private candy stash without her father knowing she was eating the candy set out for "company." To the day he died, Neville Crawford had never known that M&M's came in yellow. It had been her and her mother's secret. All the yellow M&M's were hers.

Those were some of the good memories. But there were also bad ones. Like the final week of her mother's life, when Blue had visited her in the hospital and seen how much her mother had been suffering, no matter how bravely she had smiled. Her mother had never been sick a day in her life, but within eight weeks of being diagnosed with an inoperable brain tumor, the woman who had given her life was gone. Blue had cried and cursed the shortness of time when she had been younger. Now she was glad the illness had been swift and the suffering had been over quickly.

Matt's finger lightly stroked her cheek. "You're pale."

"It's November." She wasn't about to explain how his mother's arrival had stirred buried memories within her mind. She glanced away from the concern in his eyes. "There's a lot to do and we don't have much time."

"There's nothing to do, Blue, except put away the food that will spoil. Veronica's not the fussy type when it comes to neatness. As long as the roof doesn't leak directly on her head and there's hot water for her herbal tea, she's fine."

"That's not what I was referring to." She started to yank things from the grocery bags as if her life depended on it. "I'm more worried about our sleeping arrangements."

Matt's hand froze in midair. He was clutching a

bottle of dishwashing liquid. "What about our sleeping arrangements?"

"I can't stay in your room with your mother here."

He set the yellow plastic bottle on the counter. "Why not? The last person who would pass judgment on you or me is Veronica. She believes in total freedom of the mind, body, and spirit."

Blue thought it was strange that Matt kept referring to his mother as Veronica instead of Mom. "Are you trying to tell me—how do I put this delicately?—that your mother sleeps around?"

He shook his head. "No. Veronica hasn't so much as kissed a man, that I'm aware of, since my father died." He opened the freezer and started to toss in the dozen bags of frozen vegetables Blue had unpacked. "She came of age during the radical sixties and early seventies and has traveled from one end of this nation to the other more times than I care to count." He shut the freezer door and grinned. "It would take more than you sharing my bed to raise one of her eyebrows." He took a step closer to her and comically leered at her chest. "If I had to wager a guess, I would say it would shock her if we're not sharing a bedroom."

"Well, be prepared to shock her, then." She moved around him and carried two cartons of eggs to the refrigerator. "Because there is no way I'm sharing your bed while your mother is right down the hall." Every one of her father's lectures on the sins of the flesh came back to mind in vivid detail.

Hellfire, damnation, and body-deforming diseases loomed in front of her eyes. Never mind about the unwanted pregnancies, blindness, and the stoning she would surely receive.

"Where are you planning to be sleeping, then?" Matt asked.

"The empty bedroom will do." She tossed yogurt, margarine, and a bag of shredded mozzarella cheese into the refrigerator.

"Don't be ridiculous, Blue, it doesn't even have a bed." He grabbed her arm as she hurried back toward the counter. "Honestly, she probably won't even think twice about where you're sleeping."

"I'm your housekeeper, Matt. Housekeepers don't sleep with their employers."

He ran his fingers through his hair. "You're not my housekeeper, Blue."

"Then what exactly am I?" She really would love to know the answer to that one. She'd be the first to admit she was one sorry excuse for a housekeeper, but she had managed to get Matt to every one of his doctor's appointments or anywhere else he'd needed to be during the past few months. He had cooked more meals than she, and every time she'd entered the kitchen he'd usually been right behind her to help out. They were lovers, but that didn't mean that he *loved* her. So what exactly was she to him?

She already knew what he was to her. Matthew Stone was the love of her life. He was her heart.

Clearly frustrated, he again ran his hand

through his already tousled hair. "My mother knows you're something more than my housekeeper."

"You told her we were sleeping together?" Lord, that hurt. She knew Matt and his mother talked on the phone about once a week, but she'd never have thought he would tell her something so damn personal.

"I don't go around kissing and telling, Blue. How could you even think I would tell my mother that?"

"We do more than just kiss, Matt." She turned back to the counter on the pretense of finding something else that needed to be put away immediately. "What exactly did you tell her?"

"I told her you were special."

Special. She was someone special to Matt. It wasn't a declaration of love, but it beat a stick in the eye. "Thank you." She discovered a box of frozen fruit pops under the paper towels and placed it in the freezer. "I'm still moving out of your bedroom while your mother is here. All those years of my father's preaching weren't for nothing." She shook her head at the absurdity of it all. This was the nineties. No one cared if you had sex any longer, as long as it was *safe* sex. Matt and she had been practicing safe sex since their first night together.

He sighed heavily. "Do you want me to help move your stuff?"

She gave him a small smile. He understood. He might not agree with her decision, but he understood. "No, I can handle that. Why don't you see if you can put some of this away?" Her arm swept over the overflowing counter. She headed for the stairs, stopped, and turned around and pointed at the frozen turkey. "Oh, and see what you can do with Wonder Bird, there. He's too big for the freezer and I even have my doubts about him fitting into the refrigerator."

Matt glanced at the frozen turkey and chuckled. "Go do what you have to do, Blue. I'll handle our Thanksgiving dinner."

Matt stood at the plate-glass window and watched as the plane his mother was in descended from the night sky. Blue was standing, quietly and nervously, beside him. He had tried repeatedly on the drive to the airport to reassure her that Veronica Stone couldn't care less about sleeping arrangements. Blue hadn't bought any of it. Her clothes now hung in the spare bedroom's closet and all her personal items had been removed from his bathroom. It was as if she had never shared his bed.

He didn't think his mother was going to buy it for one minute. The instant he had told Veronica that Blue was special, his mother had known the truth. He was in love. No woman had ever been "special" before. At first Veronica had been polite and hadn't asked many questions regarding Blue. Most of their conversations had centered on his injury and his reassurances that he was fine and that

Blue was taking excellent care of him. But during the last few weeks, Veronica had brought Blue's name up with more frequency. She had even hinted at a possible visit. A topic, for the first time in his life, he had avoided. He'd never minded his mother's visits in the past, but with Blue living with him, the rules had changed. He wanted Blue and his mother to meet, one day, but not quite yet.

His relationship with Blue was too intimate. Too new. Too special to be subjected to outside influences. He didn't know where he stood with Blue and he didn't want any witnesses to his own doubts.

He watched as the plane taxied to a stop and the jetway extended to the door. He placed his arm around Blue and gave her a quick hug. "Everything is going to be okay."

"Who's worried?"

She was, Matt almost told her. Instead, he said, "Veronica's one of the easiest persons in the world to get along with. Nothing fazes her." Which sounded great, unless you happened to be her son.

Passengers began entering the terminal through the jetway, and Matt moved them over so they could see the people coming. Blue repositioned herself half a foot away from him, too far for him to keep his arm around her. He frowned at her move, but didn't comment. He might understand Blue's reluctance to advertise their feelings, but it didn't mean he had to agree with it. He nodded toward the jetway. "There she is."

Blue craned her neck to see through the open

door of the gate. Among the many passengers walking through the jetway, she had no trouble spotting Veronica Stone. She looked exactly like her picture, right down to the smile. Veronica must have spotted Matt, because she waved. The wave seemed to include her, too, so Blue raised her hand and waved back with Matt.

Matt took the opportunity to grab her hand. "Come on, Blue, try to relax." He smiled at her. "But if Veronica asks for your birth date and time, don't give it to her. She'll have your astrological chart drawn up within hours. And whatever you do, don't let her talk you into trying some of her specially blended tea. It's lethal."

Blue freed her hand from Matt's just as his mother entered the terminal and threw herself into his arms. Matt must have known the enthusiastic greeting was coming, because he caught her weight in one arm and without staggering.

"Matthew, you look wonderful." Veronica pulled back and ran her gaze from the top of his head to the tip of the cane. "I expected worse." She glanced at Blue. "You must be Beulah, and I owe you a debt of gratitude for taking care of my son." She held out her hand.

Blue had no choice but to accept the hand and the friendly smile. "My friends call me Blue, and no gratitude is necessary." She felt herself relax as Veronica gently squeezed her hand.

"You have my undying thanks, even though Matthew insisted his injury wasn't too severe." She brushed a kiss across Matt's cheek. "I see all the prayers we've been chanting have helped." She glanced down at the cane. "Very debonair, son."

Matt grinned at his mother. "It's not staying. The doctor assured me that by mid-December, the cane will be a thing of the past."

"Good. Have you been using the ointment I sent?" She took charge of the little group and headed them in the direction of baggage claim.

"Only when absolutely necessary, like after a strenuous hike. Whatever is in that foul-smelling stuff works wonders on my aching muscles."

"You were supposed to be using it twice a day, Matt." She kept one eye on the luggage carousel and one eye on her son. "How are you going to get better if you don't do what I say?"

"I am getting better." He winked at Blue. "Do I want to know what's in the ointment?"

"Some things are better left to the imagination, son." She nodded at a purple knapsack making its way around the carousel. "I did add mint to try to mask some of the worst odors for you."

Matt grabbed the knapsack and set it at his feet. "I noticed the mint."

Blue hid her smile by glancing away. She had smelled the ointment Matt was referring to and had to agree. Adding mint to it was like spritzing a pile of cow dung with Chanel No. 5; totally ineffective.

Veronica pointed at a large leather suitcase before turning to Blue. "You have been fixing his tea just the way I had written?"

"Tea?"

"Now, Veronica . . ."

"Matthew Stone, do you mean to tell me you didn't give Blue the tea I sent?"

"I loathe tea, and you know it." He placed the suitcase by his feet but refused to meet his mother's gaze. "Is this it?"

"Yes, and don't change the subject."

Blue bit her lip to keep from laughing. Matt looked like a little boy who'd been caught with his hand in the cookie jar and was bravely trying to bluff his way out. She liked Matt's mother. Really liked her. The next couple of days were beginning to look brighter.

She reached around Veronica and snatched up the leather suitcase before Matt insisted that he could carry it. The mother-and-son reunion was on, and she was quite content to be an innocent bystander. It was fascinating to watch Matt interact with Veronica. He obviously loved her very much. But they tended to act as friends and equals instead of parent and child. Then again, who would class Matt as a child? He was thirty-four years old and six foot two inches tall. Child he was not.

"Blue, I'm carrying that," he said as he reached for the suitcase.

"No, you aren't. I don't need you reinjuring your leg." She hurried toward the exit. "It's not that heavy." By the weight of the thing she would guess that Veronica had packed at least three frozen turkeys. All larger than the one they had back at the house.

Blue bumped and lugged the suitcase across baggage claim and out the door. Matt scowled, picked up the knapsack, and followed her. Veronica glanced between the two of them and smiled a radiant and all-knowing smile.

TEN

Blue watched as Veronica slid two pumpkin pies into the oven and set the timer. The woman was amazing. In the twenty-four hours she had been there, she had orchestrated a Thanksgiving feast fit for a king. It was a real shame Veronica was a vegetarian.

For dinner that night Veronica had made spaghetti with tiny meatballs that had practically melted in Blue's mouth. Veronica herself had eaten the noodles and a salad that appeared to have been made from geranium and dandelion leaves.

"How did you learn to cook so well," Blue asked, "especially since you hardly eat anything you make?" She would sell her soul to Lucifer to learn how to make those meatballs.

Veronica laughed as she cleaned off the counter while Blue loaded the dishwasher. "I wasn't always a vegetarian, Blue. I worked as a short-order cook in

Atlanta, a baker's assistant in Dallas, and once I even took over the head chef's job at a fancy oceanfront restaurant in Carmel, California, while he was on vacation."

"Matt told me you two traveled quite a lot when he was growing up."

"I'm sure he didn't put it so nicely." Veronica frowned at the dishcloth in her hand. "Matt didn't like being hauled from one town to the next."

"And you didn't like to stay in one spot."

Veronica looked at Blue and gave her a small smile. "Back then it used to make a lot more sense than it does now. When Matt was a boy, I couldn't stay in one spot. I needed to keep moving, to keep searching for some answers I was so sure were out there."

"Did you find your answers?"

"No. Some answers aren't in one particular place; they come from within." Veronica shook her head as if she were dislodging distant memories. "I thought Matt would benefit from seeing the country. I was wrong about that too."

"Are you sure?" Travel was something Blue had always dreamed about doing. She had been twenty-seven years old before she had crossed the Iowa state line. When she was a little girl she would have bartered more than her soul to see an ocean, a mountaintop, or anyplace that wasn't plowed under to make room for more cornfields.

Veronica glanced around the cozy kitchen and smiled. "Matt bought himself a small sliver of this country and planted his roots. Those roots go very deep, Blue. Matt would never leave his home now that he has one."

"He was prepared to live ten months in Germany."

"No one was more surprised than I that he agreed to take that job. The only reason I could come up with was he wanted that feather in his cap so he could stay here and work out of the house more. He hates the occasional traveling his profession demands."

"You could be right, but I think it had to be something more. He was supposed to be in Germany nearly a year, not his usual week here or three days there. Maybe his roots aren't as deep as you think."

"I wish I could agree with you, Blue, but I know my son. He had his whole life planned out the day he graduated from high school. College, career, house, more career, and then a wife and children."

Blue stared at Veronica and felt every ounce of color leave her face. *Matt wanted a wife and children!* "Matt wants a wife and children?"

Veronica returned her stare for a moment before turning away and wiping down the already clean counter. "He's having three."

When she could catch her breath, Blue choked out, "Three what? Wives? Kids?"

"Kids."

Matt was going to have three children! How did his mother know how many children her son was going to have? Matt had never mentioned wanting children, but then again, why would he? She was, after all, just his housekeeper. Someone who was there only temporarily. Someone who would be leaving by Christmas. "How do you know how many children he'll have?" Had Matt actually told his mother he wanted three children?

"I believe that's what his chart said. I know it said he would be in his thirties before I became a grandmother, but I'm getting a mite impatient and Matt *is* in his thirties."

"You want to become a grandmother?" Veronica didn't look old enough to have a son Matt's age, let alone become a grandmother.

"Sure. Doesn't every woman?"

Blue wasn't sure about that. How was she supposed to know what other women felt when she'd spent so little time around other women? She only knew what she felt. If she wasn't going to have a family of her own, it would be pretty safe to assume becoming a grandmother would never enter her mind. "I wouldn't know, Veronica. I haven't had a lot of contact with other women."

"Matt mentioned that your mother died when you were young and that your father raised you until he became ill and then you took care of him."

"Yes." What more could she say? Veronica had summed up her life in one easy sentence.

"It must have been hard on you being left with all that responsibility at such a young age."

"Sometimes one is given no choice but to cope

the best she can." She gave Veronica a small smile. "You of all people should know and understand that."

Matt entered the kitchen in time to hear Blue's comment. "What should Veronica know and understand?" he asked. His mouth watered at the delicious aroma of baking pumpkin pies. He had been in his office finishing up some last-minute paperwork so he could spend the next couple of days with his mother and Blue. He walked over to the wall oven, flipped on the light, and glanced inside.

His mother laughed. "We were discussing how difficult it is to keep you fed."

He glanced from his mother to Blue and knew Veronica had just fibbed. They hadn't been discussing his eating habits, and for some reason they didn't want him to know what they had been talking about. Interesting, but he'd go along with them for now. "Do I get dessert tonight, or are you both going to make me suffer?" He placed his arm around his mother's shoulders, but kept his gaze on Blue. "I'm warning you both that if I have to go to bed hungry, those pies will be gone by morning."

Veronica laughingly brushed his arm away. "Threats? Matthew Michael Stone, you should be ashamed of yourself. Those pies are for Thanksgiving dinner tomorrow." She turned to the refrigerator. "You're in luck, though. I brought some mint jelly and oat crackers with me." She pulled a small mason jar containing green jelly from the refrigerator, then reached up into one of the cabinets. "I also packed a new blend of tea that you both must try."

Matt groaned and eyed the jelly with suspicion. "Mom . . ."

Veronica filled the teakettle with water and laughed, glancing at Blue. "He only calls me mom when he wants to get out of something. But it won't work this time, Matt. I made the jelly myself and I even helped Andy blend the tea."

"Andy owns the shop next to Veronica's," Matt explained to Blue. "He's in his late fifties and looks like some 'Deadhead' who's still time-warping in the sixties. When I visited in the spring he was wearing tie-dyed T-shirts, three earrings, and an eye patch."

"Don't make fun of his patch. He has a lazy eye and he has to wear the patch so many hours a day." Veronica carefully measured out the tea.

Blue took down three cups and placed them on the table. "He sounds fascinating."

"He is." Veronica gave Matt a look that dared him to argue with her.

Matt just stared at his mother. There was something in her voice when she talked about Andy that hadn't been there before. The two of them had seemed close when he had visited. Now he was curious as to how close. "How's Andy's paper doing?" He turned to Blue. "Andy writes and distributes a New Age newsletter along with operating the local bookstore."

"It's a little more complicated than that, Matt,"

Veronica said. "Every month the newsletter grows both in size and distribution. He had to hire Lainy Todd to help part-time in the store." Veronica carefully arranged the crackers on a plate. "This summer and fall he had *Newsweek*, *Time*, and three major newspapers reprint an article of his."

Matt listened to both his mother's words and the way she had said them, and he knew. There was something more than friendship between Veronica and Andy. "Sounds like Andy is onto something."

Veronica raised one eyebrow. "Maybe he's always been 'onto something' and it just took this long for the rest of the world to catch on."

Blue chuckled. "She might have you there, Matt."

"She probably does, but don't encourage her, Blue. There'd be no living with her."

Blue grinned as she sat down at the table. "I don't plan on living with her."

Veronica laughed as she poured the boiling water into the tea server. "She has you there, Matt. Now sit down and try Andy's and my latest tea."

Matt glanced at the globby green jelly and the crackers that looked less appealing than hamster food and knew he had to at least try them. He might have gotten away without drinking Veronica's tea when she was two thousand miles away, but it would take a minor miracle to be able to refuse her when she was sitting across the table from him. He glanced at Blue, who seemed to be enjoying his mother's visit enormously. He'd rather save any minor miracles for later. He had a feeling he might need them.

He took one last sniff of the pies baking away. At least Veronica believed in cooking the traditional Thanksgiving meal. She might not eat the turkey any longer, but she still enjoyed seeing one on the dinner table. He and Blue could, if they had to, live on the leftovers for the rest of Veronica's visit.

With a sinking feeling in his stomach and a smile on his face, Matt resigned himself to Veronica's idea of dessert.

Blue stared at the blank computer screen and wondered where to begin. She had a paper due for her American literature class, but she just wasn't in the mood to write about Steinbeck's *The Grapes of Wrath*. She had more important things on her mind. Matt wanted a wife and children!

So where did that leave her?

Sighing, she sat back and stared at the clock on Matt's desk. It was two in the morning and she had promised Veronica she would meet her in the kitchen at seven to help stuff Wonder Bird. She should be sleeping, but all she had managed to do was toss and turn in Matt's sleeping bag. At one-thirty she had left the bedroom and headed for Matt's office. She might as well accomplish something, since she was up anyway.

For the past half hour she had been staring at the gray screen and thinking of nothing but Matt and his mother's words. She felt as if her dream had just ended, but then she couldn't figure out what dream that had been. She didn't have dreams concerning Matt. Did she? What had they been doing all this time besides living together? There had been no commitment, from either Matt or herself. It was supposed to be so simple.

She wasn't supposed to fall in love. She wasn't supposed to feel this empty ache deep inside her heart when she thought about Matt wanting children. She wasn't supposed to visualize dark-haired little boys with lopsided smiles.

"Penny for your thoughts."

Blue jumped and stifled a scream, then turned to the door and glared at Matt. "Lord, Matt, you scared the tar out of me."

He stepped into the room and softly closed the door. "What are you doing up?"

She shrugged. "Same as you, I guess."

"I doubt that." He grinned and walked toward her.

Blue didn't trust that hungry gleam in his eye. "Why do you doubt it?"

"Because if you'd left your bed for the same reason I did, you would have ended up in my bed, where you belong, instead of down here in the office staring at a computer."

"Oh . . ." Basically she had left her bed for the same reason as Matt, but she wasn't about to admit it to him. The man already had two women in the house fawning over him. Plus it didn't change the fact that his mother was sleeping in the bedroom next to his. She gave Matt a seductive smile. "Miss me?"

"What do you think?" He leaned his hip against the table, but didn't touch her.

He looked sexy as hell in a pair of unsnapped jeans and nothing else. She didn't know what she wanted to run her fingers through first, the tousled hair on top of his head, or the dark curls blanketing his chest. "I don't want to think any longer. I've been doing too much of it lately."

He raised an eyebrow. "What have you been thinking about? I'm sure school has you pulled in ten different directions, but my gut's telling me it's something more."

"Your gut is probably telling you the same thing mine's telling me: Your mother's tea could make even my coffee taste good."

He chuckled. "I did try to warn you, Blue."

"It wasn't that bad until I mixed it with mint jelly and oat crackers." She worried her lower lip for a moment before adding, "I really like your mother."

"I told you you would." He reached out and smoothed her lip with his thumb. "What has you so worried?"

"Who said I was worried?"

"Nobody had to say anything, Blue. I think I know you well enough to know when something is upsetting you." He brushed a soft kiss over the same spot his thumb had just caressed. "Talk to me, Blue."

What could she say? She couldn't very well demand to know if he was planning on getting married and having three children. Veronica had seemed awfully sure that whatever she had seen in his chart would come true. The thought of marriage frightened her, and the mere idea of having children terrified her. What if she became sick or helpless? Matt would be stuck taking care of her, and whatever he might have felt for her would die under the strain. What if she became a burden to her children? She couldn't do that to the people she loved.

Matt's roots were buried deep within the mountains of Vermont, while she looked at every move she made as a great adventure. The adventure had been dimming somewhat, but she still wanted to see a great many things. She wanted to swim in the Pacific Ocean, listen to jazz while walking down Bourbon Street in New Orleans, and raft down the Colorado River. She and Matt were complete opposites and had no right or reason to be together. But for now they were, and she wouldn't, couldn't, cut short the time they had left.

She needed Matt more than ever.

She swiveled her chair around so her knees pressed up against his legs. "I don't want to talk." Her fingers teasingly skimmed the waistband of his jeans.

He raised his eyebrows. "What do you want to do, then?"

She grinned and pulled her nightshirt off over her head. The soft white cotton shirt landed behind her. "I've never made love on a chair before," she said, grinning as she shimmied out of the sweatpants she'd put on earlier.

Matt studied the chair for a moment. "That might have to wait for some other time, Blue. The manufacturer of that particular chair didn't have that activity in mind when they designed it." He glanced at the desk behind him and, with one quick sweep, sent the papers scattering onto the carpet. His clock, computer terminal, and an empty coffee mug were pushed to the far end of the massive oak desk. "Will this do?"

She couldn't prevent the laugh that bubbled up as she stood and pressed herself against Matt. "That would depend."

His hands cupped her bottom and brought her in closer contact with his growing arousal. "On what?"

She rubbed the sensitive tips of her breasts against his chest as she covered his chin with tiny kisses. "If I get top or bottom."

Matt held her head still so he could capture her mouth. "You may have anything you want."

She allowed him to kiss her deeply before pulling back and asking, "Anything?" The visions that crossed her mind were scandalous and she was dying to try every last one of them with Matt.

He bent down to capture one of her hardened nipples in his mouth. The last coherent word either of them uttered for a very long time was his promise, "Anything."

Matt found his mother alone in the kitchen enjoying a cup of her tea, which smelled like boiled bark and oak leaves to him. Blue had just left for work. She was working the late shift at Jack's and wasn't due home until nearly midnight. This was the first chance he and his mother had had to be alone since her arrival three days earlier. Thanksgiving had come and gone with plenty of delicious turkey sandwiches as reminders.

He helped himself to the last cup of coffee still hot from dinner and sat down. "Care for some company?"

Veronica smiled. "Your company, always."

"You're only saying that because I'm your son."

"Possibly, but I also happen to like you. Did Blue get off okay?"

"Yes, and thanks for giving us a few moments of privacy." He stood up, grabbed a basket overflowing with mixed nuts, and sat back down. He held up a walnut and the nutcracker. "Want one?"

"Please." Veronica smiled as he split the shell. "You do that like your father."

"My father?"

"What other father would I be talking about? Mike always lined up the cracker with the seam of the nut so it split evenly."

Matt stared at the nut and split shell nestled in

his palm. "He did?" He glanced at his mother in wonder. She rarely mentioned his father. "What else do I do like him?" He was very curious about the man who had faded from his memory.

"You have his eyes, nose, and chin. But I'm afraid you got my hair."

"What's wrong with my hair?"

"Nothing, Matt. It's just that Mike had brown hair so dark, it was nearly black. It was so soft and had this natural wave most women would kill for. I used to tease him about it."

The sadness that dulled her eyes pulled at his heart. He wondered how long a person mourned. Michael Stone had lost his life nearly thirty years ago. "You loved him very much, didn't you?"

Veronica smiled. "More than life itself." She toyed with the delicate handle of her teacup. "I don't know if I should tell you this or not, but I think you have the right to know. I wanted to die so badly back then. I didn't know how I was going to go on living without him. I thought of suicide the way other people think about what to watch on television."

"What stopped you?"

"You." She gave him one of her beautiful smiles, the kind that lit up her eyes. "Every time I looked at you, I saw him. I couldn't leave you alone in the world, and I wasn't going to take you with me. So I walked around for years being torn in two."

"Why didn't you seek professional help? I'm sure the military would have provided some type of counseling." His mother had wanted to die, but he, unknowingly, had prevented it. It was a sobering thought.

"I didn't trust the military, not like your father did. He laid down his life for Uncle Sam, while I blamed them for his death. I didn't want to be brainwashed by some shrink with stripes on his shirt. I didn't want to hear how Mike was some hero. All I knew was Mike was gone and I was left to carry on alone."

"So we left the base in California."

"I thought a new town would do us some good and help dull the pain and the memories."

"When it didn't, we moved again." For the first time he began to understand what his mother must have been going through. Why hadn't he seen her pain?

"Again and again." She picked up another walnut and handed it to him. He immediately cracked it and handed it back. "I thought the constant moving would do you good. You know, let you see America. But I was wrong about that too."

"I'll admit, I wasn't thrilled with being yanked from one school to the next with barely any time to make friends. But I can't say it hurt me any."

"You can't?" She nibbled on a nut and studied her son.

"No, why? Do you think it did?"

"You've made a wonderful home for yourself and have done extremely well in your chosen career."

"Why am I hearing a *but* in there, Veronica? You've never been one to mince your words or hide your feelings before. So say it."

"You have roots here in Vermont, Matt. Deep roots."

"Go on." He knew about his roots. After all, he was the one who'd planted them. "Do you have something against roots?"

"No, roots are good, Matt. This is a lovely place to settle down and raise a family. It's the deeper roots that you have sown that worry me. They seem to go right into this mountain and I'm afraid they might not be bendable."

"Now you're confusing me. Some roots are good and others are bad?"

"In a nutshell"—she held up half a walnut shell to lighten the moment—"that's about it. Some people, Matt, are afraid of roots. They're scared of the responsibilities those roots represent. People get hurt by those roots, Matt. They could strangle a person, or set their world spinning when the root is broken. Mike was my root, and when it was torn from the ground, I was left unanchored. For a long, long time I never wanted to go anywhere near another root."

Matt stared at his mother for a long time without speaking. She had just told him two very important things. One, that she had finally accepted the loss of his father and that she wasn't afraid to take another chance. But more important, she was warning him about Blue.

Was Blue afraid of his roots? He could well imagine her father's illness and the years she had spent nursing him had been like a stranglehold. Maybe his mother was right. Maybe Blue thought love and suffocation were one and the same.

He'd have to give it some thought later. Right now there was something else that needed his attention. "Are you trying to tell me that you're thinking of putting down some roots of your own?"

"I bought the shop almost two years ago."

"I know, but you told me it was temporary, that the owner had to sell immediately and that you just happened to be there."

"True. At first I wasn't sure if I would like staying in one place and being committed to a clock."

"And now?"

"Now I'm finding I want more. The answers I've been searching for have always been with me, I was just too scared to look inside myself to see them. Since settling in Tranquility, I've found the answers, and while I don't like some of them, I can at least accept them now."

Matt reached out and clasped her trembling hand. "And where does Andy fit in all of this?" He hadn't been mistaken the other night; something was going on between his mother and Andy.

"He's a very dear friend."

He raised one eyebrow. "A friend?" The blush staining his mother's cheek gave another answer.

"He's more than a friend, Matthew." She squeezed his hand and smiled. "Do you mind?"

"Mind! Why should I mind?" He returned the squeeze and smile. "Just answer me one question."

"If I can."

"Does he make you happy?"

"Yes. For the first time in years I can honestly say, I'm happy."

He reached for her other hand and grinned. "Then all I can say is go for it!"

ELEVEN

"What do you mean, we're going skiing?" Blue mumbled sleepily, two weeks after Thanksgiving break and Veronica's departure.

"You know, clean mountain air, exercise, pure fun," Matt said.

She rolled over under the quilt and peeked at the window. "I hate to disillusion you, Matt, but you're having a dream. It's still nighttime. Come back to bed."

He chuckled as she pulled the quilt up over her head. "Rise and shine. It's four-thirty, time to get up."

Sleep-laden eyes peered at him from over the edge of the quilt. "In case you've forgotten, I don't know how to ski."

"Then today's your lucky day. I'm going to teach you."

She saw the determination written across his

face and changed tactics. "Matt, darling, dearest, love of my life, standing on toothpicks going sixty miles an hour down a mountain isn't my idea of exercise. Smashing into trees, digging bark out of my face, and spitting out snow isn't my idea of fun. It sounds more like suicide."

"They are skis, not toothpicks, and I wouldn't dream of allowing you to go sixty miles an hour your first day on the slopes. We'll take it easy." He wanted Blue to see and experience one of the benefits of living in Vermont.

"Are you sure your leg is up to it, even though the doctor gave you a clean bill of health yesterday? Speaking of which, that was really quite depraved what you did last night."

Matt gave a sinister chuckle. "I know. I've had that idea for quite a while. All I was waiting for was that clean bill of health. Besides, I don't remember you protesting too much."

She could feel the blush sweep up her cheeks and decided to drop the subject of last night. "I can't go skiing, I don't have a thing to wear." She pulled the quilt over her head again and closed her eyes, pretending to go back to sleep.

The weight of a box being dropped onto her stomach made her sit straight up. "What the . . ." She blinked sleep out of her eyes and stared at the huge white box tied with a gigantic red bow. She sent a questioning glance toward Matt, who was sitting on the edge of the bed.

"It's an early Christmas present. I picked it up last night while you were working at Jack's."

With trembling fingers she slid the bow off the box and opened the lid. Mounds of tissue paper wrapped whatever lay inside. She unfolded the top piece and revealed a pink knitted hat. Beneath that was a pair of thick pink gloves. A pink-and-purple-striped scarf followed. With an amused look, she dug deeper and came up with purple ski pants that boasted a pink stripe down each side. A thick turtleneck sweater in the same color scheme followed. The last item in the box was a purple down-filled ski jacket, complete with a lift ticket attached to the zipper.

Modesty fled as she tried on the jacket, then threw her arms around Matt. She felt him flinch as the cold metal zipper connected with his bare chest. "Oh, Matt, thank you." She placed a string of kisses up his throat to the vicinity of his mouth. "I'll be a regular snow bunny." She had always wanted to try skiing, but the cost was too steep for her meager budget. If Matt had gone through all the trouble and expense to purchase this outfit for her, wouldn't it stand to reason he was expecting her to stick around, especially through the winter?

Matt chuckled at the picture she made in his arms. He wanted to go to his grave remembering her just like this. She was totally naked except for the unzipped ski jacket. "Just remember you're my ski bunny." He captured her lips and lowered her back down onto the warm sheets.

❖━━━❖

Matt glanced at Blue and grinned. Ever since their first skiing lesson the week before, she had been buried under a mountain of schoolwork, cramming for exams. Today was the first time he had been able to talk her into leaving the office or taking her nose out of some book. Blue was bound and determined not only to pass her exams, but to graduate with honors. He had resorted to blackmail to get her to go Christmas-tree hunting with him. If she came, she could pick out the tree; if he went alone, he would get a tree less than two feet tall.

Blue was now dressed in long johns, jeans, and one of his old flannel shirts, two pairs of socks, boots, hat, gloves, ski jacket, and a scarf. She was so layered, she could barely move. "I'm telling you, Blue, you're going to sweat in all that clothing."

"It's freezing out here. Iowa gets cold winters, but it's nothing compared to this." She kicked her boot and sent a cloud of white snow into the air. "I bet you there's half a foot of snow already on the ground."

"It's only a couple of inches." The warm weather they'd had at the beginning of the week had melted everything that had been on the ground. Last night's snowfall had left the air crackling fresh and everything covered in a brilliant white blanket. "Come on, Nanook of the North, let's go get our Christmas tree." He swung the ax over one shoulder, grabbed her hand, and headed off the back deck and into the woods.

White puffs of frosted air escaped their lips with every breath they took. They trudged silently over a small bridge he'd had built and headed deeper into the woods. Matt loved the silence of his home, the freshness of the air, the scent of the woods. His long walks these past months had given him the exercise he needed, but they had also given him time to think about Blue and their future. A future Blue seemed reluctant to talk about. A future he was bound and determined they would have.

More than a few times since his mother had left, he had tried to broach the subject of their future, only to have Blue change the topic immediately. She had to go to work, she had to study, she had to do the laundry. The excuses were endless, but not his patience. She was no longer his housekeeper. They shared the housework and the cooking. Blue had even purchased an old Chevy that had seen better days, but ran like a charm. He was free to come and go as he pleased. Blue was free to come and go. He could usually be found at home. Blue ran from Jack's, to school, to home. Always running. Always on the move. It was as if she was afraid to stay in one spot too long.

Was that what his mother had been referring to? Blue's constant movement, and his determination to stay at home, to be a homebody. He loved his house and mountain. The roots he had planted in Greenhaven were as strong as the mountains that surrounded the small town.

He loved being Blue's lover, but he wanted more. He wanted her to marry him, to make a commitment, to become his family. Lately he had been experiencing horrible dreams in which he walked endlessly through his home, from room to room, calling Blue's name. She wasn't there. She was gone. He'd wake up in the middle of the night drenched in sweat and reaching for her. He didn't know how much longer he could go on like this. He understood the pressure she was under at school, so he was leery about bringing up the subject of their future again. But come Christmas . . .

He squeezed her hand. "My mother told me that my father loved the outdoors. She said I got my love of nature from him, while she's more of a people person."

"Which one did you inherit your computer talent from?"

"Had to be my father. Veronica said he loved logic, that everything had an order. She swears he saw the world in black-and-white. Everything could be measured. It was or it wasn't."

"I'll take a guess here and say your mother sees the world as gray. And I don't think I'd be going out on a limb by betting she even believes in ghosts and other creatures that go bump in the night."

Matt chuckled. Veronica believed in more than just ghosts. She swore people had auroras, past lives, and destinies. "They were complete opposites, yet whatever they had must have been something very special."

Blue frowned and whispered, "While it lasted."

He pulled her to a stop and turned her to face him. Was that what she was afraid of, that it wouldn't last? "We have something very special, Blue." He wondered what she would do if he blurted out his love and his dreams of a future together. Would she run and hide, or would she stay?

"Yes, we do." She reached out and touched his cheek with a snow-coated mitten. "Let's not spoil it by fighting."

"Fighting is the last thing I want to do with you, Blue." She still wasn't ready to hear him. He nodded in the direction of a small clearing. "We're here."

Blue looked around and grinned. "I can pick any one?" She started to walk around every tree there.

"Remember that we have to drag it back and that the living-room ceiling is only eight feet high." Most of the trees were well over that height and he didn't relish the idea of dragging some twenty-foot tree the quarter mile back to his house.

It took her a few minutes, but Blue narrowed it down to two trees. "Which one do you think?"

"Both would make excellent Christmas trees, but choose that one." He pointed at a seven-foot Douglas fir.

She looked at the tree he'd pointed to and slowly did another turn around it. "Why this one?"

"It's sandwiched between two larger trees. It

doesn't have a very good chance to grow to its full potential. The other one is far enough away to have that chance."

She grinned. "A body like that, and a brain. Lord, I am impressed."

He wiggled his eyebrows. "You said something to that effect last night, if I'm not mistaken." He picked up the ax, and with a dozen good blows, the tree crashed to the ground.

If the gleam in her eye was any indication, Blue was about to make another smart-mouth remark when something caught her attention. "Look, Matt, a cat."

He turned and was surprised to see an orange tiger cat sitting primly on an old decaying log. "Blue, meet Moondancer."

"She's the one who brings the *presents?*"

Matt chuckled at the astonishment in Blue's voice. He couldn't blame her, though. Moondancer looked like she could star in a television commercial eating out of a crystal dish set on a linen napkin. "She's the one. Looks can be deceiving."

Blue watched the dainty orange-striped cat gracefully wash her paw. When the job was done to the animal's satisfaction, she flashed sparkling green eyes and purred. "How could you be so cruel as to leave her outside?" Blue demanded.

"You saw some of her presents. Do you really think she needs protection?"

"She doesn't look like a vicious killer to me."

He looked back at Moondancer and had to

agree. "I know. Let me tell you that these woods used to be filled with all kinds of animals. Now they are few and far between. I even think the deer are thinning out."

Blue burst out laughing. "Be serious, Matt. Do you think she'd let me pet her?"

"She might. She knows you've been feeding her." He was astounded that Moondancer was still there looking at them as if expecting some sort of praise.

"How does she know that?" Blue took a few cautious steps toward the cat.

"She knows everything that goes on around here." He watched as Blue stopped in front of the log and slowly reached out her hand. Moondancer delicately sniffed the mitten. When no teeth sank into the red mitten, he released his breath and relaxed further when Blue started to scratch Moondancer behind the ears.

A contented purr reached his ears and he smiled. Blue made almost an identical sound after they'd made love and she was snuggling up against him in bed. "She likes you." He handed Blue the ax and started to drag the tree back to his house.

Blue followed with the playful cat dancing between her feet. Billowing puffs of snow scattered wherever Moondancer went. Matt glanced behind him occasionally and smiled all the way back to the house. What a pair they made. Both proud, independent females so afraid to be loved, yet needing it so desperately.

Moondancer would probably have perished if it hadn't been for his help, especially during the winter months. He knew she sneaked into the garage on cold winter nights to bunk down in a box filled with clean rags he'd left there for her. Moondancer wasn't going to change into some cuddly domesticated pet that spent her evenings curled up in front of a roaring fire.

But he had hope for Blue. She had to love him. There was no other explanation for the way she responded to his every touch.

He leaned the tree against the house and watched Blue frown as Moondancer stayed at the edge of the woods.

"Doesn't she ever come in like Raven?"

"No. The only time she comes to the house is at night. Then it's only to eat and leave a gift." He saw the sadness clouding her eyes. "She'll be okay, Blue. I promise." He pulled her into his embrace and gave her a quick hug. They both glanced at the edge of the woods. Moondancer had disappeared. "Let's go get a cup of hot chocolate and warm up."

Blue stared at the circled advertisement in the newspaper clutched in her hand, then back at the house in front of her. This was the place. *Studio apartment for rent. Some furniture. Utilities included.* The monthly rent was reasonable, which to her budget meant it was so low that at first she thought the paper had made a misprint and quoted a weekly rate. She had called the number listed, just to make sure.

The house in front of her appeared to be in need of a fresh coat of paint and a good gardener. It looked like half a forest of pine trees was growing in the front yard. Some industrious soul had wrapped each tree with multicolored Christmas lights. The rest of the yard was decorated with three plastic sleds, eight Santas, a seven-foot plastic snowman, and a herd of reindeer. Christmas carols were blaring from the loudspeakers attached to the porch railing. Any minute now she expected to see little elves scurrying across the snow-covered front yard.

She glanced up and down the street and concluded that all things considered, she was lucky. The house was in a nice section of Greenhaven, not far from the college. Jack's Diner was only a fifteen-minute car ride away. It looked like a cheerful place to live, but it wasn't Matt's home. She had grown to love the peace and quiet of his mountain. Grown to love his company, his smile, his touch. Grown to love him more with each passing day.

It was time, past time, to take a step away from him. To put some distance between them so she could start to control her rebellious thoughts and dreams. She had no business dreaming of things that could never be. Marriage, babies, and a family of her own had no place in her future. She had vowed never to allow their stranglehold into her life again. So why were the dreams feeling like love and not suffocation?

Today she had completed her last exam for the semester. Her agreement with Matt was ended. It was time to move on, while she still had the strength. With a determined smile she stepped around a child's sled, over a pair of hockey sticks, and made her way up the shoveled walkway toward the house.

TWELVE

Matt woke from his dream with a start and automatically reached for Blue. His hand encountered a warm sheet, but no Blue. His eyes flew open as he glanced around the dark room. No Blue, either in the room or the adjoining bathroom. Something was wrong. He had known it earlier. Felt it like a physical force when she had returned home earlier that evening.

She had been late getting back from school, and whatever had been troubling her, she hadn't wanted to talk about it. They had eaten dinner, cleaned up, then Blue had done something she had never done before. She had asked him to make love to her.

How could he refuse?

He had felt almost a desperation in her when he had taken her in his arms. They never made it past the living room. After their quick release, he had carried her up the stairs to his bed, where he made slow delicious love to her once more. They had both fallen asleep in total exhaustion and satisfaction. Or so he had thought.

Matt got out of bed, slipped on a pair of jeans, and went in search of Blue. He found her in the dark kitchen, sitting by the window, staring out back. "Blue?"

She didn't turn to face him. "Moondancer didn't leave a present tonight."

He walked into the room and took a seat near her. She had pulled on one of his shirts. The sleeves were rolled up half a dozen times, and the hem fell to her knees. She looked as lost in his shirt as she did sitting in his dark kitchen. "You saw her?"

"Both her and Raven." He noticed she was holding something in her hand. It appeared to be a rolled-up newspaper. "They were here about an hour ago."

His concern deepened. Blue had been sitting alone in the dark for over an hour. "You've been up for quite a while. Do you feel okay?"

"I'm fine, Matt. I needed time to think."

"About?"

"The past, the present, and the future."

He tried to make her smile. "Sounds like a Dickens book I read once."

"Don't worry. No ghost weighted down with chains visited the bedroom tonight. Tiny Tim will survive." Blue toyed with the paper in her hand. "I was trying to figure out the best way to tell you something."

"Tell me what?" Why wouldn't she turn around and look at him? There was more light outside with the full moon and freshly fallen snow than there was in the kitchen.

"I decided straight to the point would be best."

Matt felt his heart slide up into his throat when she reached up and appeared to wipe her eyes. Was Blue crying? Her voice had the husky note of tears, but she wasn't sniffling or sobbing. "Blue, you're scaring me. What's wrong?"

"Nothing's wrong, Matt. I took my last final today and you don't need my help around the house any longer, so our deal is concluded."

"What—"

She held up the paper to silence him. "Let me finish, please." This time he was positive she was wiping away tears. "On the way home from school I stopped at an apartment that was for rent. It's a little on the small size, but it's clean and freshly painted."

"Now wait just one minute, Blue." He stood up. "Are you telling me you're leaving?"

She touched the pane of glass with her fingertips. "It's close to the college, and not too far from Jack's." Her voice broke with every word, with every step he took closer. "The rent is reasonable and it is partially furnished."

Matt reached for the light switch and flooded the room with light. He wanted to see her face. Needed to see her face. "Why, Blue?"

"I can't stay here any longer, Matt. Our deal is concluded."

"Screw the deal, Blue."

She flinched, but didn't back down. "I'm sorry. . . ."

He grabbed her chin, and forced her to look at him. The pain etched in her face tore at his heart, but he was fighting for his life now. Without Blue, he would have no life. "Stay."

She shook her head. "I can't."

Her tears wet his fingers, which were still cupping her chin. He was losing her. "I'm not very good with flowery speeches or pretty words, Blue. I interface better with a computer than another human. But there's something I should have told you a long time ago. I love you." He released her chin and brushed at the steady stream of tears pouring down her cheeks. "I was going to wait until Christmas to ask you."

"Ask me what?" Her words were so softly spoken, he had to read them from her lips.

"Will you marry me and become my wife?" This wasn't how he had planned it. He had visualized something more romantic. Sitting in front of a fire with only the Christmas tree and flames for light. Maybe some sweet wine and hot kisses. And the ring. He hadn't forgotten the ring. It was upstairs hidden between his summer shorts where she wouldn't find it.

He watched as what little color she had in her

cheeks faded to pale white. Her lips trembling, she whispered, "Wife?"

"Yes, wife. Marriage, maybe a couple children, you know, the American dream."

"You're going to have three."

"Three what?"

"Children. Veronica told me you will have three children."

Matt sighed. "So that's what's been upsetting you. You once told me that you weren't going to have any children." He brushed a kiss across her lips. "Ignore my mother and her astrological rantings. If you don't want any children, we won't have any." He would gladly give up his dream of children if it meant having Blue. In the fantastic world of dreams, children were the icing on the cake; Blue *was* the cake.

She shook her head and pulled back. "That's not it, Matt."

"What's not it? Children?"

She scooted back farther and stood up. "I just can't marry you."

"Why not?" He closed the gap between them and lightly grasped her shoulders. "Do you love me, Blue?" Everything inside his heart told him that she did. So why was she running? He had expected some sort of response, that she would either joyously throw herself at him declaring her love, or she would deny it. He hadn't expected the reaction he was getting.

He was totally floored when she blocked both

her ears with her hands and started to shake violently. "Blue?"

"He used to ask me that all the time. 'Do you love me, Beulah? Stay and show me how much you love me. It's your duty to stay. Honor thy father and mother, Beulah; it's the Lord's commandment.'" She opened her eyes and stared at Matt as if she had just discovered something. "Why do you suppose it's honor thy father and not love thy father?"

"I don't know." He swallowed the lump of tears that had formed in his throat. Now he understood. To Blue, love was not the rose, but the thorns. If he tried to hold her tight to his heart, she would throw herself against the thorns of love and slowly bleed to death. To Blue love was a trap, and if he begged, pleaded, or demanded that she stay and take a chance on him, he might as well spring the trap himself. Their love would be doomed.

He didn't know if he had the strength to let her go, but he knew he had to. Blue's father had held her for ten years by using words of love, honor, and duty. All words that were traditionally used when referring to marriage. No wonder Blue was torn up inside. On the one hand, she loved him and wanted a life together; on the other, she remembered what love had cost her in the past. He recalled a saying he'd heard—if you love something, set it free; if it returns, it was meant to be.

He opened up his arms and gathered her close to his heart. "It's okay, Blue." Her tears branded his chest, but he held her fast and gave her her freedom. "If you really want to live in town, I won't stop you." He cupped her chin and forced her to look at him. "I won't pretend to like the idea, but I understand."

"You do?" She blinked back another flood of tears. "How could you understand when I don't?" Her fingers trembled against his cheek as she stroked his face. "I love you, Matt."

He smiled. Those were the words he had been praying for. Somehow, someway, things were going to work out. They had to. "I know." She was only moving into Greenhaven, a mere twenty-minute drive away. He had an entire semester before she graduated to make her see that love was not a chain, but a set of wings. He was a patient man. And a persistent one. Blue loved him. He could wait.

He swept her up into his arms and headed out of the kitchen. "Come back to bed and I'll show you what you'll be missing." Golden curls tickled his shoulder and he felt her mouth press against his throat. Desire flared quickly and his body hardened in anticipation of loving Blue. Sparks! They still struck sparks off each other.

Blue stared out her apartment window at the falling snow and wondered what in the hell she was doing there. Four days and three frustrating nights she had been away from Matt, and she could do nothing but think of him and his proposal. He wanted her to become his wife! He wanted a family!

She should be singing with joy and shouting from the rooftops. Instead, she had cried herself to sleep every night. Matt had let her go without so much as a word after their conversation in the kitchen that night. She had packed her bags the next morning and he had helped carry them to her car. She had driven away with the memory of Matt standing on the snow-blanketed porch watching her leave.

She closed her eyes and once again she could taste the last kiss they had shared. She could feel Matt's arms around her, pulling her closer to his warmth, closer to his heart.

Her eyes popped open as her breath quickened. She was fantasizing about a man who was half a mountain away. She was in bad shape and it was showing.

All morning and afternoon long Jack had been giving her strange looks as she waited on tables. Half the orders she had taken were wrong. It was a good thing that it was Christmas Eve and that most of the people who had stopped into the diner while doing last-minute Christmas shopping had been forgiving. The tips she had received were generous, the looks sympathetic, and Jack had asked her twice if she was feeling okay. No, she wasn't feeling okay. Her heart was breaking minute by minute and it was her own stupid fault.

While pouring Mrs. Bethsman her second cup of coffee, she had realized that she had placed Matt's love in the same category as her father's. The two men were nothing alike. Her father had been demanding, nasty, and downright spiteful. What could he have known of love? He hadn't known how to give it or receive it. Neville Crawford had died a lonely, bitter old man. How could she have compared that man with Matt?

Matt loved her enough to set her free. He had said that he'd give her the time she needed to think, but didn't that mean he had time to think also? What if he'd changed his mind in the past couple of days? What if he'd decided he didn't love her after all? She was a fool.

She had watched young married couples, old married couples, and lovers come and go all day long at the diner. None of them had seemed to be strangling to death in the relationship. Even old Ed Moonly, who griped and complained while his wife, Kate, changed his entire lunch order to a low-fat, more healthy meal, had winked at Blue behind his wife's back. He had known how much he was loved even if he preferred the pork-roast platter over turkey breast on whole wheat.

Now that she thought about it, even Caleb Willing, back in Iowa, wasn't strangling to death. Working himself to death, maybe, but not strangling. He was working the farm out of love, both for his family and the land. He could have made other choices, but he hadn't. Caleb had tried to explain that to her years ago, but she hadn't listened. Hadn't been ready to listen.

She was ready now, if only it wasn't too late. She

wanted Matt to be her husband and she wanted to be the one who gave him those three children. She wanted a family of her own, where love would never hurt, only heal.

Blue turned away from the window and walked to the bed, where a single present lay. Matt's present. It was the first Christmas present she had bought in two years, since her father had passed away. On the way home from work she had stopped at a men's clothing shop. In the window was a green sweater she had been admiring for weeks. It had taken all of today's generous tips and then some, but she had purchased the sweater and had it gift-wrapped.

She had been going to wait until tomorrow to take it to him, but she couldn't wait any longer. The snow was falling more heavily now. By tomorrow the roads up the mountain might be too dangerous for her car. She needed to go now, or chance being cut off from Matt for days.

Matt glanced at the kitchen table in front of him and grinned. His mind had finally snapped. He was in the middle of compiling Blue's last Christmas present. A couple of days ago he had spotted a porcelain bowl hand-painted with brilliant wildflowers, Blue's favorite, and hadn't been able to resist buying it for her. Wrapping an empty bowl hadn't sat right with him, so that morning he had purchased every bag of M&M's from the local Shop-N-Bag. For the last twenty-five minutes he had been separating the yellow candy from the rest and placing them into the bowl. The bowl was three quarters full, and he was almost out of bags.

He had no idea why Blue preferred the yellow candy over the other colors; they all tasted the same to him. But if Blue liked the yellow, then that was what she was going to get. He missed her terribly, but he had kept his word and given her time. Tomorrow she would be out of time. He was coming down off his mountain, bearing gifts and a proposal.

The last four days and three lonely nights had driven home the fact that she was his life. He couldn't sleep, couldn't eat, and concentrating on work had been a joke. He had driven by her apartment so many times, he was surprised no one had called the police and reported a stalker. The storm raging outside was going to slow him down come morning, but he was prepared. He had already checked the Bronco and the plow attached to the front. He was ready for anything under four feet of snow. It was going to take more than the predicted ten inches to keep him from Blue tomorrow.

Matt dumped another handful of yellow candy into the bowl just as someone pounded on his front door. What idiot was out in the middle of a storm? On Christmas Eve, no less. It was probably Jared, making rounds and needing a cup of hot coffee. Jack's Diner had closed for the holidays after the lunch shift. Matt left the kitchen and headed for the living room.

He flipped on the porch lights and opened the door. The wind howled and snow flew into his face and the room. A five-foot two-inch snowflake dropped a box and stumbled into his arms. "Blue," he cried, both from the shock of her being there and the coldness of her coat. He slammed the door shut against the storm.

She tried to talk, but all she could accomplish was the chattering of her teeth.

He muttered a curse and quickly dragged her to the burning fire. He peeled off her snow-crusted hat, mittens, and scarf as she just stood there staring at the flames. "What happened?" He brushed her damp curls away from her red face and pale lips.

When she simply stared at him, he cursed again and tugged off her jacket and boots. Her jeans were soaked and caked with snow, so he unsnapped them and pulled them off her legs. Damp socks and her sweatshirt were the next things to go. When she was standing in front of the fire wearing nothing but her panties and bra and a thousand goose bumps, he cursed once more.

He pulled the afghan from the back of the couch and wrapped her tightly in its warmth. After dragging a chair as close to the fire as he dared, he lowered Blue into it. "I'll go get you something warm to drink." He had checked her fingers, toes, and other extremities for signs of frostbite and he was pretty confident she was okay on that score.

Within minutes he was back with a steaming

mug of hot chocolate. He knelt in front of her and held the mug out. "Blue, you should drink this."

She reached for the mug, and he noticed her hands were still trembling, but not nearly as badly as before. "Thanks, I think my jaw has thawed." She took the mug with both hands and sipped the drink.

Matt watched her, but didn't say a word. He was afraid that if he opened his mouth he would start yelling and demanding to know what she was doing out on a night like this. Didn't she realize the dangers? She could have lost some fingers and toes to frostbite. She could get pneumonia and end up in the hospital. She could have been lost and . . . He didn't want to finish that thought, but he could have lost her tonight.

She handed him the empty mug. "Go ahead and yell, Matt. I can see that you want to, and believe me I deserve it."

Maybe his mother was right, he thought. Maybe there were such things as angels. He closed his eyes and gave a silent prayer of thanks to whatever angel had been looking over Blue tonight. "Tell me what happened first. Then I'm going to yell."

"I looked worse than I really was." He only raised one eyebrow at her assessment of the situation. "I was almost here when my car hit a drift on your drive. I couldn't go forward or back, so I had to walk." She clutched the blanket together at her throat. "I only had to walk a couple hundred yards."

"Up a dark driveway in the middle of a blizzard?"

"It's not a blizzard, Matt. And I drove that driveway enough times to know how to follow it to get to your door." She reached out and touched his jaw. "I know now it was a foolish thing to do, but I had to see you tonight."

He captured her still-cold hand and pressed it to his lips. "What's so important that you would risk your life?"

"I didn't think I was risking my life, Matt." She nodded toward the door and the package lying in front of it. "It's Christmas."

He glanced at the clock on the mantel. "Not for another five hours." He turned and looked at the semicrushed present lying on the floor. "I hope it wasn't breakable."

"It wasn't." *My heart is, though,* Blue added silently. Now that she had defrosted and the hot chocolate had melted the hunk of ice that had been in her belly, she was feeling foolish. She was sitting in her panties and bra, wrapped in a blanket, and praying Matt would propose again. Why would he? He had asked her to marry him once, and she had turned him down. Matt wasn't stupid or a glutton for punishment. She had a feeling that if there was going to be any asking, it would have to come from her.

She nervously toyed with the fringe on the afghan. "I'm afraid of loving you, Matt."

He smiled. "I know."

"But I'm more afraid of losing you." She took his hand and held it tight. "All my life love has hurt, Matt. I don't want to be hurt again."

He pulled her out of the chair and onto the floor with him. "I can't promise never to hurt you, Blue." He brushed a curl off her cheek. "But I can promise never to hurt you intentionally."

"Do you mind a wife who is still in college?" She didn't want to give up her dream again in the name of love. She was so close, she could almost feel that diploma in her hands.

"I think it's wonderful that you have dreams and ambitions, Blue. It's part of who you are, and I love all of you."

"Would you mind a wife who opens her own preschool?"

Again he shook his head and smiled. "If you were home all day I'd never get anything done. I'd be too busy making love to you all day long."

"Hmmm . . . Maybe I'll reconsider opening that preschool after all."

He grabbed her around the waist and pushed her down onto the thick carpet. Grinning, he loomed over her. "Any other questions before I ravish you?"

She liked the sound of that. She had never been ravished before, or at least not knowingly. But there was still one important question she had to ask. She had to know just how far Matt would let her dream. "What happens if I have to move away from this area to work in the child-care field? What if Greenhaven isn't large enough to support another preschool? What if I have to move up to Burlington, or to New York, or even Arizona?"

Matt studied her face for a long time before answering. "Then we move."

"You would leave your mountain for me?"

"I would move a mountain for you, Blue. What's selling a piece of property compared to losing you?"

She felt humbled and loved all at the same time. She would never ask Matt to sell his mountaintop or move, for she had grown to love it as much as he. Just knowing he would was love enough. Tears of happiness filled her eyes as she gazed up at the man she loved. "I have one more favor to ask, Matt."

"Anything."

"Repeat your proposal so I can say yes." She'd tell him later about the three children she had always dreamed about. "I know you wanted to ask me on Christmas, but I can't wait a moment longer. I've waited a lifetime for you."

He wiped away a tear that had escaped the corner of her eye. "Will you marry me, Blue, and become my wife?"

She wrapped her arms around his neck and pulled his mouth down to hers. "I thought you'd never ask."

❖————————❖

Blue and Matt welcomed in Christmas in front of the blazing fire with only the flames and the Christmas tree for light. There was sweet wine, hot kisses, and yellow M&M's. And a diamond ring gleaming on the third finger of Blue's left hand, and the promise of forever glowing in their eyes.

THE EDITORS' CORNER

February is on the way, which can mean only one thing—it's time for Treasured Tales V! In our continuing tradition, LOVESWEPT presents four spectacular new romances inspired by age-old myths, fairy tales, and legends.

LOVESWEPT favorite Laura Taylor weaves a tapestry of love across the threads of time in **CLOUD DANCER**, LOVESWEPT #822. Smoke, flames, and a cry for help call Clayton Sloan to the rescue, but the fierce Cheyenne warrior is shocked to find himself a hero in an unknown time. Torn by fate from all that he loves, Clay is anchored only by his longing for Kelly Farrell, the brave woman who knows his secret and the torment that shadows his nights. In this breathtaking journey through history, Laura Taylor once more demonstrates her unique storytelling gifts in a moving evocation of the healing power of love.

A chance encounter turns into a passionate journey for two in **DESTINY UNKNOWN**, LOVESWEPT #823, from the talented Maris Soule. He grins at the cool beauty whose grip on a fluffy dog is about to slip, but Cody Taylor gets even more pleasure from noticing Bernadette Sanders's reaction to his down and dirty appearance. Common sense tells the sleek store executive not to get sidetracked by the glint in the maverick builder's eyes. But when he seeks her out time and time again, daring to challenge her expectations, to ignite her desire, she succumbs to her hunger for the unconventional rogue. Maris Soule demonstrates why romantic chemistry can be so deliciously explosive.

From award-winning author Suzanne Brockmann comes **OTHERWISE ENGAGED**, LOVESWEPT #824. Funny, charismatic, and one heck of a temptation, Preston Seaholm makes a wickedly sexy hero as he rescues Molly Cassidy from tumbling off the roof! The pretty widow bewitches him with a smile, unaware that the tanned sun god is Sunrise Key's mysterious tycoon—and one of the most eligible bachelors in the country. He needs her help to fend off unwanted advances, but once he's persuaded her to play along at pretending they're engaged, he finds himself helplessly surrendering to her temptation. As fast-paced and touching as it is sensual, this is another winner from Suzanne Brockmann.

Last but not least, Kathy Lynn Emerson offers a hero who learns to **LOVE THY NEIGHBOR**, LOVESWEPT #825. The moment she drives up in a flame-red Mustang to claim the crumbling house next door, Marshall Austin knows he was right. Linnea Bryan is bewitching, a fascinating puzzle who can easily hold him spellbound—but she is also the daughter of the woman who destroyed his parents' marriage. So he launches his campaign to send her packing. But even as he insists he wants her out of town by nightfall, his heart is really saying he wants her all night long. Kathy Lynn Emerson draws the battle lines, then lets the seduction begin in her LOVESWEPT debut!

Happy reading!

With warmest wishes,

Beth de Guzman

Shauna Summers

Beth de Guzman   Shauna Summers

Senior Editor   Editor

P.S. Watch for these Bantam women's fiction titles coming in February: Available for the first time in paperback is the *New York Times* bestseller **GUILTY AS SIN** by the new master of suspense, Tami Hoag. Jane Feather, author of the nationally bestselling *VICE* and *VALENTINE*, is set to thrill romance lovers once again with **THE DIAMOND SLIPPER**, a tale of passion and intrigue involving a forced bride, a reluctant hero, and a jeweled charm. And finally, from Michelle Martin comes **STOLEN HEARTS,** a contemporary romance in the tradition of Jayne Ann Krentz in which an ex–jewel thief pulls the con of her life, but one man is determined to catch her—and never let her get away. Don't miss the previews of these exceptional novels in next month's LOVE-SWEPTs. And immediately following this page, sneak a peek at the Bantam women's fiction titles on sale *now*!

For current information on Bantam's women's fiction, visit our new web site, *Isn't It Romantic,* at the following address: **http://www.bdd.com/romance**

Don't miss these terrific novels
by your favorite Bantam authors

On sale in December:

HAWK O'TOOLE'S HOSTAGE
by Sandra Brown

THE UGLY DUCKLING
by Iris Johansen

WICKED
by Susan Johnson

HEART OF THE FALCON
by Suzanne Robinson

Sandra Brown

Her heady blend of passion, humor, and high-voltage romantic suspense has made her one of the most beloved writers in America. Now the author of more than two dozen New York Times bestsellers weaves a thrilling tale of a woman who finds herself at the mercy of a handsome stranger—and the treacherous feelings only he can arouse. . . .

HAWK O'TOOLE'S HOSTAGE

A classic Bantam romance available in hardcover for the first time in December 1996

To Hawk O'Toole, she was a pawn in a desperate gamble to help his people. To Miranda Price, he was a stranger who'd done the unthinkable: kidnapped her and her young son from a train full of sight-seeing vacationers. Now held hostage on a distant reservation for reasons she cannot at first fathom, Miranda finds herself battling a captor who is by turns harsh and tender, mysteriously aloof, and dangerously seductive.

Hawk assumed that Miranda, the beautiful ex-wife of Representative Price, would be as selfish and immoral as the tabloids suggested. Instead, she seems genuinely afraid for her son's life—and willing to risk her own to keep his safe. But, committed to a fight he didn't start, Hawk knows he can't afford to feel anything but contempt for his prisoner. To force the government to reopen the Lone Puma Mine, he must keep Miranda at arm's length, to remember that she is his enemy—even when she ignites his deepest desires.

Slowly, Miranda begins to learn what drives this brooding, solitary man, to discover the truth about his tragic past. But it will take a shocking revelation to finally force her to face her own past and the woman she's become . . . and to ask herself: Is it freedom she really wants . . . or the chance to stay with Hawk forever?

"Only Iris Johansen can so magically mix a love story with hair-raising adventure and suspense. Don't miss this page-turner."—Catherine Coulter

THE UGLY DUCKLING

by *New York Times* bestselling author

Iris Johansen

now available in paperback

Plain, soft-spoken Nell Calder isn't the type of woman to inspire envy, lust—or murderous passion. Until one night when the unimaginable happens, and her life, her dreams, her future, are shattered by a brutal attack. Though badly hurt, she emerges from the nightmare a woman transformed, with an exquisitely beautiful face and strong, lithe body. While Nicholas Tanek, a mysterious stranger who compels both fear and fascination, gives her a reason to go on living. But divulging the identity of her assailant to Nell might just turn out to be the biggest mistake of Tanek's life. For he will soon find his carefully laid plans jeopardized by Nell's daring to strike out on her own.

He had come for nothing, Nicholas thought in disgust as he gazed down at the surf crashing on the rocks below. No one would want to kill Nell Calder. She was no more likely to be connected with Gardeaux than that big-eyed elf she was now lavishing with French pastry and adoration.

If there was a target here, it was probably Kavinski. As head of an emerging Russian state, he had the power to be either a cash cow or extremely troublesome to Gardeaux. Nell Calder wouldn't be considered troublesome to anyone. He had known the answers to all the questions he had asked her, but he had wanted to see her reactions. He had been watching her all evening, and it was clear she was a nice, shy woman, totally out of her depth even with those fairly innocuous sharks downstairs. He couldn't imagine her having enough influence to warrant bribery, and she would never have been able to deal one-on-one with Gardeaux.

Unless she was more than she appeared. Possibly. She seemed as meek as a lamb, but she'd had the guts to toss him out of her daughter's room.

Everyone fought back if the battle was important enough. And it was important for Nell Calder not to share her daughter with him. No, the list must mean something else. When he went back downstairs, he would stay close to Kavinski.

> *"Here we go up, up, up*
> *High in the sky so blue.*
> *Here we go down, down, down*
> *Touching the rose so red."*

She was singing to the kid. He had always liked lullabies. There was a reassuring continuity about them that had been missing in his own life. Since the dawn of time, mothers had sung to their children, and they would probably still be singing to them a thousand years from then.

The song ended with a low chuckle and a murmur he couldn't hear.

She came out of the bedroom and closed the door

a few minutes later. She was flushed and glowing with an expression as soft as melted butter.

"I've never heard that lullaby before," he said.

She looked startled, as if she'd forgotten he was still there. "It's very old. My grandmother used to sing it to me."

"Is your daughter asleep?"

"No, but she will be soon. I started the music box for her again. By the time it finishes, she usually nods off."

"She's a beautiful child."

"Yes." A luminous smile turned her plain face radiant once more. "Yes, she is."

He stared at her, intrigued. He found he wanted to keep that smile on her face. "And bright?"

"Sometimes too bright. Her imagination can be troublesome. But she's always reasonable and you can talk to—" She broke off and her eagerness faded. "But this can't interest you. I forgot the tray. I'll go back for it."

"Don't bother. You'll disturb Jill. The maid can pick it up in the morning."

She gave him a level glance. "That's what I told you."

He smiled. "But then I didn't want to listen. Now it makes perfect sense to me."

"Because it's what you want to do."

"Exactly."

"I have to go back too. I haven't met Kavinski yet." She moved toward the door.

"Wait. I think you'll want to remove that chocolate from your gown first."

"Damn." She frowned as she looked down at the stain on the skirt. "I forgot." She turned toward the bathroom and said dryly, "Go on. I assure you I don't need your help with this problem."

He hesitated.

She glanced at him pointedly over her shoulder.

He had no excuse for staying, not that that small fact would have deterred him.

But he also had no reason. He had lived by his wits too long not to trust his instincts, and this woman wasn't a target of any sort. He should be watching Kavinski.

He turned toward the door. "I'll tell the maid you're ready for her to come back."

"Thank you, that's very kind of you," she said automatically as she disappeared into the bathroom.

Good manners obviously instilled from childhood. Loyalty. Gentleness. A nice woman whose world was centered on that sweet kid. He had definitely drawn a blank.

The maid wasn't waiting in the hallway. He'd have to send up one of the servants from downstairs.

He moved quickly through the corridors and started down the staircase.

Shots.

Coming from the ballroom.

Christ.

He tore down the stairs.

WICKED

by Susan Johnson

"An exceptional writer."—*Affaire de Coeur*

Serena Blythe's plans to escape a life of servitude had gone terribly awry. So she took the only course left to her. She sneaked aboard a sleek yacht about to set sail—and found herself face-to-face with a dangerous sensual stranger. Beau St. Jules, the Earl of Rochefort, had long surpassed his father's notoriety as a libertine. Less well known was his role as intelligence-gatherer for England. Yet even on a mission to seek vital war information, he couldn't resist practicing his well-polished seduction on the beautiful, disarmingly innocent stowaway. And in the weeks to come, with battles breaking out on the Continent and Serena's life in peril, St. Jules would risk everything to rescue the one woman who'd finally captured his heart.

"Your life sounds idyllic. Unlike mine of late," Serena said with a fleeting grimace. "But I intend to change that."

Frantic warning bells went off in Beau's consciousness. Had she *deliberately* come on board? Were her designing relatives even now in hot pursuit? Or were they explaining the ruinous details to his father instead? "How exactly," he softly inquired, his dark eyes wary, "do you plan on facilitating those changes?"

"Don't be alarmed," she said, suddenly grinning. "I have no designs on you."

He laughed, his good spirits instantly restored. "Candid women have always appealed to me."

"While men with yachts are out of my league." Her smile was dazzling. "But why don't you deal us another hand," she cheerfully said, "and I'll see what I can do about mending my fortunes."

She was either completely ingenuous or the most skillful coquette. But he had more than enough money to indulge her, and she amused him immensely.

He dealt the cards.

And when the beefsteaks arrived sometime later, the cards were put away and they both tucked into the succulent meat with gusto.

She ate with a quiet intensity, absorbed in the food and the act of eating. It made him consider his casual acceptance of all the privileges in his life with a new regard. But only briefly, because he was very young, very wealthy, too handsome for complete humility, and beset by intense carnal impulses that were profoundly immune to principle.

He'd simply offer her a liberal settlement when the *Siren* docked in Naples, he thought, discarding any further moral scruples.

He glanced at the clock.

Three-thirty.

They'd be making love in the golden light of dawn . . . or sooner perhaps, he thought with a faint smile, reaching across the small table to refill her wineglass.

"This must be heaven or very near . . ." Serena murmured, looking up from cutting another portion of beefsteak. "I can't thank you enough."

"Remy deserves all the credit."

"You're very disarming. And kind."

"You're very beautiful, Miss Blythe. And a damned good card player."

"Papa practiced with me. He was an accomplished player when he wasn't drinking."

"Have you thought of making your fortune in the gaming rooms instead of wasting your time as an underpaid governess?"

"No," she softly said, her gaze direct.

"Forgive me. I meant no rudeness. But the demimonde is not without its charm."

"I'm sure it is for a man," she said, taking a squarely cut piece of steak off her fork with perfect white teeth. "However, I'm going to art school in Florence," she went on, beginning to chew. "And I shall make my living painting."

"Painting what?"

She chewed a moment more, savoring the flavors, then swallowed. "Portraits, of course. Where the money is. I shall be flattering in the extreme. I'm very good, you know."

"I'm sure you are." And he intended to find out how good she was in other ways as well. "Why don't I give you your first commission?" He'd stopped eating but he'd not stopped drinking, and he gazed at her over the rim of his wineglass.

"I don't have my paints. They're on the *Betty Lee* with my luggage."

"We could put ashore in Portugal and buy you some. How much do you charge?"

Her gaze shifted from her plate. "Nothing for you. You've been generous in the extreme. I'd be honored to paint you"—she paused and smiled—"whoever you are."

"Beau St. Jules."

"*The* Beau St. Jules?" She put her flatware down and openly studied him. "The darling of the broadsheets . . . London's premier rake who's outsinned his father, The Saint?" A note of teasing had entered her voice, a familiar, intimate reflection occasioned by the numerous glasses of wine she'd drunk. "Should I be alarmed?"

He shook his head, amusement in his eyes. "I'm very ordinary," he modestly said, this man who stood stud to all the London beauties. "You needn't be alarmed."

He wasn't ordinary, of course, not in any way. He was the gold standard, she didn't doubt, by which male beauty was judged. His perfect features and artfully cropped black hair reminded her of classic Greek sculpture; his overt masculinity, however, was much less the refined cultural ideal. He was startlingly male.

"Aren't rakes older? You're very young," she declared. And gorgeous as a young god, she decided, although the cachet of his notorious reputation probably wasn't based on his beauty alone. He was very charming.

He shrugged at her comment on his age. He'd begun his carnal amusements very young he could have said, but, circumspect, asked instead, "How old are *you?*" His smile was warm, personal. "Out in the world on your own?"

"Twenty-three." Her voice held a small defiance; a single lady of three and twenty was deemed a spinster in any society.

"A very nice age," he pleasantly noted, his dark eyes lazily half-lidded. "Do you like floating islands?"

She looked at him blankly.

"The dessert."

"Oh, yes, of course." She smiled. "I should save room then."

By all means, he licentiously thought, nodding a smiling approval, filling their wineglasses once more. *Save room for me—because I'm coming in.* . . .

Blazing with romance, intrigue, and the splendor of
ancient Egypt

HEART OF
THE FALCON

The bestselling

Suzanne Robinson

at her finest

*All her life, raven-haired Anqet had basked in the tran-
quillity of Nefer . . . until the day her father died and
her uncle descended upon the estate, hungry for her land,
hungry for her. Desperate to escape his cruel obsession, she
fled. But now, masquerading as a commoner in the magnificent city of Thebes, Anqet faces a new danger. Mysterious and seductive, Count Seth seems to be a loyal soldier to
the pharaoh. Yet soon Anqet will find that he's drawn her
back into a web of treachery and desire, where one false
move could end her life and his fiery passion could brand
her soul.*

Anqet waited for the procession to pass. She had
asked for directions to the Street of the Scarab. If she
was correct, this alley would lead directly to her goal.
She followed the dusty, shaded path between win-
dowless buildings, eager to reach the house of Lady
Gasantra before dark. She hadn't eaten since leaving
her barber companion and his family earlier in the
afternoon, and her stomach rumbled noisily. She

hoped Tamit would remember her. They hadn't seen each other for several years.

The alley twisted back and forth several times, but Anqet at last saw the intersection with the Street of the Scarab. Intent upon reaching the end of her journey, she ran into the road, into the path of an oncoming chariot.

There was a shout, then the screams of outraged horses as the driver of the chariot hauled his animals back. Anqet ducked to the ground beneath pawing hooves. Swerving, the vehicle skidded and tipped. The horses reared and stamped, showering stones and dust over Anqet.

From behind the bronze-plated chariot came a stream of oaths. Someone pounced on Anqet from the vehicle, hauling her to her feet by her hair, and shaking her roughly.

"You little gutter-frog! I ought to whip you for dashing about like a demented antelope. You could have caused one of my horses to break a leg."

Anqet's head rattled on her shoulders. Surprised, she bore with this treatment for a few moments before stamping on a sandaled foot. There was a yelp. The shaking stopped, but now two strong hands gripped her wrists. Silence reigned while her attacker recovered from his pain, then a new string of obscenities rained upon her. The retort she thought up never passed her lips, for when she raised her eyes to those of the charioteer, she forgot her words.

Eyes of deep green, the color of the leaves of a water lily. Eyes weren't supposed to be green. Eyes were brown, or black, and they didn't glaze with the molten fury of the Lake of Fire in the *Book of the Dead*. Anqet stared into those pools of malachite until, at a call behind her, they shifted to look over her head.

"Count Seth! My lord, are you injured?"

"No, Dega. See to the horses while I deal with this, this . . ."

Anqet stared up at the count while he spoke to his servant. He was unlike any man she had ever seen. Tall, slender, with lean, catlike muscles, he had wide shoulders that were in perfect proportion to his flat torso and long legs. He wore a short soldier's kilt belted around his hips. A bronze corselet stretched tight across his wide chest; leather bands protected his wrists and accentuated elegant, long-fingered hands that gripped Anqet in a numbing hold. Anqet gazed back at Count Seth and noted the strange auburn tint of the silky hair that fell almost to his shoulders. He was beautiful. Exotic and beautiful, and wildly furious.

Count Seth snarled at her. "You're fortunate my team wasn't hurt, or I'd take their cost out on your hide."

Anqet's temper flared. She forgot that she was supposed to be a humble commoner. Her chin came up, her voice raised in command.

"Release me at once."

Shock made Count Seth obey the order. No woman spoke to him thus. For the first time, he really looked at the girl before him. She faced him squarely and met his gaze, not with the humility or appreciation he was used to, but with the anger of an equal.

Bareka! What an uncommonly beautiful commoner. Where in the Two Lands had she gotten those fragile features? Her face was enchanting. High-arched brows curved over enormous black eyes that glittered with highlights of brown and inspected him as if he were a stray dog.

Seth let his eyes rest for a moment on her lips. To watch them move made him want to lick them. He appraised the fullness of her breasts and the length of her legs. To his chagrin, he felt a wave of desire pulse through his veins and settle demandingly in his groin.

Curse the girl. She had stirred him past control. Well, he was never one to neglect an opportunity. What else could be expected of a barbarian half-breed?

Seth moved with the swiftness of an attacking lion, pulling the girl to him. She fit perfectly against his body. Her soft flesh made him want to thrust his hips against her, right in the middle of the street. He cursed as she squirmed against him in a futile effort to escape and further tortured his barely leashed senses.

"Release me!"

Seth uttered a light, mocking laugh. "Compose yourself, my sweet. Surely you won't mind repaying me for my inconvenience?"

On sale in January:

GUILTY AS SIN
by Tami Hoag

THE DIAMOND SLIPPER
by Jane Feather

STOLEN HEARTS
by Michelle Martin